the women of hearts book five

MARCI BOLDEN

CHEATING HEARTS

ISBN-13: 978-1-950348-73-2

the women of hearts book five

MARCI BOLDEN

CHEATING HEARTS

PINK SAND
PRESS

PROLOGUE

Lisa Steele ran from her car toward her apartment building as the winter wind cut right through her thin coat and sleet started spitting down, painfully pelting her face and hands. She held what was left of her medium deep-dish sausage and black-olive pizza in one hand and her camera bag in the other.

She'd learned the hard way that camera bag straps weren't nearly as trustworthy as they should be, so she always carried the bag by the sturdy handle. The long purse strap barely clung to her shoulder as she rushed over the slick ground in her high-heeled boots, silently begging the universe to help her keep her balance with every step.

One of these years, she'd accept that heels and winter weather didn't go well together. This didn't look like the year.

Approaching the entrance of the old brick building, she debated the easiest way to dig her keys from her pocket to swipe the fob in front of the sensor that would unlock the glass-paneled door. If she'd been thinking about more than the chill reaching her bones, she would have hooked the keys over her ring finger like she did when attempting to carry all her groceries in at once. For the thousandth time, she wished the lighting was brighter than the amber hue shining down from a post that looked like it must have been original to the 1970s construction.

The dim lighting made entering the building at night unsettling in good weather. With the current conditions, the scene felt more like a cheap horror film than the safe and welcoming entrance to the building that had been her home for more than three years.

Not much longer, she told herself. Soon she'd be able to afford to move into a nicer, safer environment. As she neared the door, someone came out and held it open for her. She frowned, but she didn't complain. This time.

Usually, she made a point of reminding her neighbors that a secure building wasn't secure if they held the door for people. There was a reason the door automatically locked. There was a reason residents had to have a fob to get inside. Holding the door open for people put their safety at risk. Why was that so hard to understand?

This night, however, in the sleet and her inadequate outer layer, she simply nodded. That was as close to *Thank you for violating the rules* as she was going to get.

Once inside the building, she shook as much of the sleet from her hair as she could. As soon as she got upstairs, she was going to get out of her wet clothes and take a hot shower. She was so cold, her teeth were starting to chatter.

Her scowl returned when she stopped in front of the

elevator. A strip of silver duct tape secured a bright-yellow sheet of paper with a handwritten note to the elevator door.

OUT OF ORDER

The head of maintenance had promised the building tenants the elevator would be fixed by the end of the day. Then again, the head of maintenance made a lot of promises he rarely kept. The broken elevator, however, seemed to be the biggest annoyance yet as far as Lisa was concerned. Carrying bags up four flights of stairs, as she'd done the last three weeks, was a pain in the ass.

Rolling her head back, she attempted to blow her jet-black hair from her face, but the sleet had melted, and damp strands stuck to her forehead. She used the back of her hand securing her camera to get the hair from her eyes before turning toward the stairwell.

The cement steps were smooth from years of use, making them slippery as hell on a good day. And this was *not* a good day. There had been non-slip strips on these stairs when she'd moved in. Those were gone now, creating yet another hazard the building manager seemed to ignore.

Soon, she reminded herself. Soon she would be able to move into a nicer building.

Another chill ran through Lisa as she started up the steps. Her pizza and camera bag felt unnaturally heavy by the time she reached the second floor. This was the last straw. The last one.

Two months ago, she had threatened to write an exposé on

the slumlord overseeing her building. If he didn't fix the issues, she'd make such a fuss the local Department of Public Health would have no choice but to send an inspector—and not just to this property but all the other complexes he owned. Dragging his name through the mud would be her personal mission.

He hadn't taken her threat seriously, but she had meant it.

By the third floor, she was panting, and her calves were on fire. Going down the stairs in her heels hadn't been nearly as straining as going up. Of course, she hadn't been planning on going up because the stupid elevator was supposed to be fixed.

The moment she reached the landing that would lead to the fourth floor—her floor—the door opened. She would have smiled, genuinely thankful this time, but the person didn't hold the door for her. Actually, the door was slammed much harder than it would have closed naturally.

Startled, Lisa finally focused on the person standing in front of her as she stopped on the fourth-floor landing.

"I've been looking for you," said the unexpected visitor standing before her.

Lisa's heart sank to the pit of her stomach. There wasn't much that made her anxious. As an investigative journalist, she had developed a taste for the excitement of confrontation. However, confrontation rarely found her in the dark and creepy stairwell of her apartment building.

She started to ask how the intruder got into the building but immediately recalled how someone had held the door for her without a moment's hesitation. Damn neighbors. The lack of security was another thing she was going to complain about.

"Excuse me," Lisa said, stepping to move around the person. She scoffed when her way was blocked. *Rude!*

She stepped to the other side, once again attempting to bypass the person, but a hand grabbed for hers. Rather, grabbed the camera bag she was holding. Lisa jerked back, absolutely outraged. The feeling only lasted for a moment, however, as her drastic reaction tipped her precarious balance.

Survival instincts kicked in, and Lisa threw her arms out to get her balance. Terror rolled through her as she realized she was about to fall. Her ankle twisted awkwardly in her heeled boot, and she tumbled. There was no way to know how many stairs she hit on the way down, but she felt every one of them. Her thin, wet jacket did nothing to cushion the blows. The cement edges cut into her shoulders, her elbows, and her ribs as she rolled toward the bottom.

The real pain hit when her head slammed against the dingy, white-painted cinderblock wall. The moment her skull smashed against the hard surface, her eyes filled with bright flashes of light. She blinked hard several times, trying to focus, but the vibrations of the impact made clearing her mind impossible. The intense pain was all she could perceive.

A shadow loomed over her for several seconds before kneeling at her side. Lisa tried to ask for help, but the words wouldn't form. She moaned, or at least she thought she did. Her hand jerked as the camera bag was yanked from her limp fingers.

Don't, she thought, but the words didn't leave her.

Moments later, darkness filled her eyes, and the world went black.

[1]

Since moving into the role of private investigator at HEARTS Investigative Services, the closest Tika Brown had come to being a *real* PI was following cheating spouses or insurance scammers and testifying in court about what she'd witnessed. Before that, she had spent nearly a year helping her coworkers do research for their cases and learning the ropes. She'd had to master those skills before she'd even been allowed to follow slimeballs to cheap motels.

Prior to coming to HEARTS, she'd been studying to be an attorney. True, she had dropped out of college before she could graduate, but she had been hired as a paralegal soon afterward and had learned a lot. The knowledge she'd gained had been valuable to her team and helped her earn the confidence of her boss, Holly Austin.

Even so, Tika had to start at the bottom of the ladder before she could be assigned any *real* cases. All that changed today. Holly had said the man who'd made an appointment with HEARTS for this morning had asked for Tika specifically. Tika was so excited, a squeal had nearly escaped her when she'd found out.

However, squealing with excitement wasn't likely something Holly would have seen as appropriate. Holly hadn't even squealed when she'd gotten engaged. She'd smiled, laughed a little, and then was right back to business. Holly was the straight-arrow type. Not the jump-up-and-down-squealing-with-excitement type.

Tika had been shrieking inside her mind all morning. Every time she thought about the potential of doing an investigation that didn't involve watching married people sneak around on their spouses, a little firework of happiness exploded in her chest. She had opted to hide in her office so she didn't let anyone else in on how happy she was. Clients, after all, didn't hire HEARTS unless they were suffering in one form or another, so being this happy to work a case was something she had to learn to cover.

Every time she heard voices in the lobby, her heart rolled in her chest, and she held her breath and listened. Being the least experienced investigator on the team meant she got the dinky office closest to the distractions and coming and goings of the lobby. Today was the first day that felt like a blessing.

Finally, minutes before her scheduled appointment, Tika heard the deep baritone of a man's voice saying his name.

"Wade Steele. I have an appointment."

This is it. This is it. This is it. Oh my God!

She didn't know the details of the case—just that he suspected someone he knew had been murdered. *Murdered!* And this man had asked for her help to solve it.

Those fireworks of excitement went off again. Tika closed

her eyes, clenched her hands together, and blew out her breath. *Be cool*, she told herself.

"If you're done praying," Holly said from the door, "we have an interview to conduct."

Tika opened her eyes, ready to explain herself, but the smirk on Holly's lips proved her boss had been teasing her. That wasn't usually Holly's approach, but Tika appreciated it. Getting a stern look from Holly likely would have burst her bubble. Holly was wonderful and warm beneath her cold and serious exterior. *Far* beneath. The exterior was intimidating as hell, though, even after years of working with her.

Tika stood and wiped her palms down her slacks. "I'm ready."

She followed Holly into the HEARTS lobby where Sam, their Internet guru and team assistant, was smiling and batting her eyes ever so slightly at the man. Tika couldn't blame her. Wade Steele stood tall and self-assured at the reception desk. His crisp black suit was a shade or two darker than his hair, and both stood out against his pale skin.

When he looked at her with haunted gray eyes, she could swear his pain was out there for the world to see. The reality of what she had reminded herself of earlier hit her. He wouldn't be there if he weren't suffering in some way. She had to remember that. This was her first serious case, but it was a personal tragedy this man was suffering.

The look in his eyes humbled her and dampened her excitement. She held out her hand and smiled sweetly as Holly introduced her.

"It's nice to meet you, Mr. Steele," Tika said, even though something inside her felt as if she'd met him before. He seemed familiar for reasons she didn't understand. She scanned over his face, trying to place him, but she couldn't recall when or where their paths might have crossed.

"Ms. Brown," he said, taking Tika's hand. He smiled, and a little dimple appeared in his left cheek. His smile was soft, as if just being in her presence brought him reassurance. That was odd. So was the intense way he was staring at her.

Tika glanced at Holly, who seemed to have noticed his overt interest as well. Tika took a moment to skim over Wade's entire form—likely decoding his body language as Holly tended to do—before sweeping her arm toward the conference room.

There were two things Tika had learned about her boss over the last year. First, Holly was keenly observant. Second, she was extremely protective of her team. If something was off about Wade Steele, she'd find it in the next fifteen minutes or so of questioning him about his case. If she sensed he had ulterior motives for being there, she'd tell him they weren't the right private investigators for him and send him on his way.

Being a team of women investigators provided many benefits. They connected on a deeper level than simply coworkers, which made their bond as a team unbreakable. One of the downfalls, though, was that more than once, someone had tried to hire them to fulfill some secret female PI fantasy rather than to solve an actual case. Holly had become a master at recognizing those types and shoving them out the door without wasting too much of anyone's time.

The way Wade had looked at Tika during their introduction had clearly raised the first red flag.

Their footsteps echoed across the tiled lobby until they entered the conference room. The gray commercial-grade carpet silenced their steps as they walked toward the long oval table. Though the room looked neat and tidy at the moment, two panels on wheels hid scribbles, charts, and notes taped to the room-length whiteboard. If there hadn't been a meeting with a client scheduled, one of the other members of HEARTS would undoubtedly have had notebooks and folders scattered about the dark-stained table as she tried to solve her latest case.

And one of the HEARTS, probably Eva, would be in there eating as she pecked away on her laptop and tossed out ideas. Tika loved that about her job. Everything here was a team effort, even their cases. If she ever stumbled, got lost, or felt overwhelmed, one of her teammates would be right there to help her find her way without hesitation or casting doubt on Tika's abilities. She couldn't have asked for a better place to land after leaving college the way she had.

"Would you like some coffee or water?" Holly asked Wade as she gestured toward the chair she wanted him to take. He declined her offer as he sank into the black chair as if weighed down by whatever had brought him to HEARTS.

"We're sorry for your loss, Mr. Steele," Holly said as a segue into the reason they were sitting there.

He looked at Tika.

She put a sympathetic smile on her lips. "Very sorry," she added.

"As I explained to your receptionist when I made my appointment," Wade said, "I don't think my sister's death was an accident."

"May I ask how she passed?" Holly asked.

Wade hesitated before looking at Holly. He seemed to be questioning why she was there when his appointment was with Tika.

But Holly was the team leader. She would hear his concerns and any evidence he had obtained, and then she would determine if there was a case and if Tika was the right investigator for the job. Just because Wade had requested to work with Tika didn't mean Holly would assign her to the case or that HEARTS would take it.

And if he kept looking at Tika the way he was—like she was the only other person in the room—Holly wasn't even going to let him finish telling them why he needed their help. She would send him on his way because his interest in Tika seemed to outweigh the reasons he'd given for wanting to meet with her.

"She fell down a flight of stairs." Wade shifted, as if uncomfortable, thinking about the details. "She hit her head and broke her neck." Though his deep voice had echoed around the room before, it softened to almost a whisper by the time he finished explaining the loss of his sister.

Holly stared at him, but he didn't continue. "People slip on staircases all the time, Mr. Steele. What makes you think this was more than an accident?"

"She was a journalist. A damn good one," he said. "Lisa Steele."

Tika's heart dropped to the pit of her stomach. She was certain her umber skin must have changed at least three shades as she widened her eyes with the shock over what he'd said.

He continued focusing on Tika. "Lisa was my sister. You're the same Tika Brown she went to school with, right?"

Holly jerked her face to Tika. "You knew her?"

Knew her? Yes, Tika knew her. Lisa Steele had ruined her life.

Damn it. Now she understood the sense that she knew him when she'd first looked into his eyes. She should have made the connection the moment she'd seen his porcelain skin, dark hair, and light-gray eyes that were a near-perfect match to Lisa's.

Now that the dots had been connected for her, she could easily see the same eagerness in Wade's eyes as she'd seen when Lisa was reassuring Tika that everything was going to be *just fine.*

"Yeah," Tika managed to say. "We went to the same university. She graduated three years ago. I didn't," she stated flatly.

Wade smiled. "So you did know her."

The confirmation seemed to have soothed him somehow, and now the puzzle pieces fell into place. The strange introduction fit. He was, in fact, seeking her out. Not because of some weird *Charlie's Angels* fetish but because she knew his sister.

"She wrote the article that exposed what you were going through with some of your professors," Wade said.

Tika nodded and blew out her breath slowly to keep the anger of what Lisa had done from surfacing. "She did."

Tika didn't look at the woman sitting next to her, but in her peripheral vision, she saw Holly glance at her. Much as she had when she was quickly taking in Wade in the lobby, Holly was clearly assessing Tika's reaction.

Other than the uncontrollable way her cheeks had likely lost some color and a brief widening of her eyes at the mention of Lisa's name, Tika managed to hold herself together. Calm and cool. Just like a professional PI would be in the face of learning something unexpected.

Holly returned her attention to Wade. "Why do you think her death was suspicious?"

"We'd gone out to dinner a few days before her fall," he said. "She was agitated, and when I pressed her about it, she said she'd gotten another death threat. Not *a* death threat, but *another*."

"Did she report the threats to the police?" Holly asked.

He shook his head. "She said that kind of thing happened all the time in her line of work, and if she ever got worried, she would tell someone. She was more angry than scared."

Holly scribbled something on the notepad she had carried in with her. "Do you know if she talked to her boss?"

"Lisa was a freelance investigative journalist." The pride in Wade's voice was obvious. He clearly admired her. "She liked being able to write stories that interested her instead of being forced into assignments. She was highly respected for her work." He looked at Tika as if expecting her to confirm his statement.

Tika simply blinked at him. She thought she was smiling, but her mind was still reeling, so she couldn't be certain.

"I don't suppose she told you what she was working on?" Holly asked.

Wade sank back. "No. She always said it was bad luck to

share her work before publication. But whatever it was, I'm sure it was big," he said, once again focusing on Tika. "She took on big issues that helped people. That's what she did. Like how she helped you."

Tika somehow managed to swallow the bitter laugh threatening to erupt from her. Lisa Steele hadn't helped her. Lisa had *used* her to get a big story, and when the heat got to be too much, Lisa broke every promise she'd made to get the story in the first place. Her vow to never—under any circumstances—reveal Tika as a source was as thin as the air at the top of Mount Everest. The moment the university administration pressed, Lisa folded and sold Tika out.

Tika had been called before a review board to point her finger and make complaints about the racism she'd faced from several faculty members. The university did an investigation and removed two professors as a result. Tika was relieved that the board had taken action, but she had foolishly thought her days of feeling targeted were over.

Though the board never released her name publicly, Tika had no doubt she'd become a target in a different way. Financial aid "misplaced" her paperwork not once but multiple times. Her work-study position was "phased out," and several students seemed to have caught wind of the truth behind her troubles.

Though her family and several friends begged her to not give up, the stress of being singled out because she had spoken up became too much, and Tika withdrew from school. She'd considered simply transferring to a different college but needed to take time to recover emotionally first. That recovery time went from one semester to several years.

She ended up working as a paralegal at her brothers' law firm and listened to them tell her how she needed to go back to school. Every single day they had the same conversation. Finally, she had had enough and decided the only way to stop their lectures was to get out of law altogether.

Without a degree, she never expected to find a job that would allow her to use her knowledge, until she saw an ad for a newly forming private investigation firm hiring someone to assist with legal research. The moment she walked into the interview, she had known she'd found the place where she belonged. Holly had called her back before the end of the day to offer her a position.

A year later, Tika was ready to tackle her first big case, but she wasn't ready for that case to deal with the person she held responsible for sending her entire life spiraling out of control.

Lisa Steele's story won national collegiate awards. She had graduated that same year with honors and was praised for the brave story Tika had been foolish enough to help her write. The story that had cost Tika the future she had wanted for most of her life.

Now Lisa was dead, and her brother was staring at Tika, waiting for confirmation that Lisa had been some kind of warrior for the underdog and had helped her. Helped her? The only thing Lisa had done was cause Tika to lose everything.

Holly saved Tika from Wade's scrutiny by asking, "Did anyone see her fall?"

"No," Wade answered. "None of her neighbors heard or

saw anything. Nobody reported seeing anything out of the ordinary."

Holly made a note. "Was there surveillance footage?"

He focused on Holly again. "The building manager had been in the process of updating software, or so he says. According to what Lisa told me, he always had excuses for issues with the building and only dealt with them when he absolutely had to. She was concerned about the security in the building—or lack thereof."

"So there were other issues with the building?" Holly pressed.

Wade seemed annoyed that she focused on that instead of the lack of security. "Yes, but..." His point seemed to fade away before he could make it.

"Did you tell the police that Lisa had been threatened?" Holly asked.

"I did, but I didn't have any proof, and I couldn't find anyone to verify what she'd told me. She hadn't told her friends or anyone else in our family about the threats. Without an editor overseeing her work, she didn't have anyone to report it to. The police said there was no evidence to suggest there was more to her fall than an accident, and since she... Since she couldn't tell us what happened, other than looking for signs of defensive wounds, I don't think they looked into it."

"Were there signs of defensive wounds?" Holly asked.

"No."

Holly sighed softly. Tika heard it, but she didn't think Wade had.

"Was anything missing?" Tika asked. "Her purse or jewelry?"

Wade shook his head. "No. Her wallet was still in her bag, and she didn't usually wear jewelry."

Holly frowned. "Mr. Steele—"

Wade turned his attention to Tika again, pinning her in her seat with his light-gray eyes. "If I could just find proof that someone threatened her, the police would have to look into it, right?"

Tika hesitated before nodding. "If there was sufficient evidence to indicate she was threatened, then, yes, they'd likely look into it."

"So help me find evidence. Help me get into her files to see if there was something more to this." When Tika simply stared at him, he scoffed. "You owe it to her," he said firmly.

Tika opened her mouth, but Holly lifted her hand in a silent but effective way of stopping her from telling him exactly what she owed Lisa Steele.

"We are tremendously sorry for what you are going through," Holly stated, "but the article Lisa wrote about the racism my colleague dealt with was years ago and in no way left Tika indebted to you, Lisa, or anyone else."

Wade widened his eyes and opened his mouth as if to counter what she had said.

"I understand where you are coming from," Holly continued. "I understand your pain and the need to make sense of an unexpected loss. But that does not give you the right to try to guilt someone your sister barely knew into doing your bidding."

"I didn't..." His shoulders sagged, and he sighed as a look

of shame came to his eyes. "I'm sorry. You're right." He looked at Tika and offered her a soft smile. "After Lisa passed, I called the police detective I'd talked to about her fall. He told me there wasn't anything for him to look into. This was an accident." Desperation haunted his eyes. "I just need to know that. I need to know that she wasn't hurt on purpose. That's all. When I was looking for an investigator and found you... I thought the coincidence was a sign. I'm sorry."

Tika felt her frustration at him ease. He appeared to be so broken and discouraged. He obviously believed someone had caused Lisa's death and needed someone to hear him. To validate his concerns. Tika knew that feeling all too well. Though she had initially been furious that someone had tipped off the school paper to what she'd been dealing with, she also recalled how relieved she'd been when Lisa had promised to help.

Of course, Lisa ended up throwing Tika under the bus, but that wasn't Wade's fault. Clearly he hadn't even known about that.

He muttered something about wasting their time as he started to stand.

"Wait," Tika blurted out. "Did she tell you how she received the threats made against her?"

"No."

Tika glanced at Holly. "It wouldn't hurt to look through her emails, social media, and phone records."

"You don't have to," Holly said softly.

Tika took a breath and let it out slowly as she made her decision to help him. All he needed to ease his mind was someone to help him determine if his sister had been intentionally hurt. She wasn't absolving Lisa's bad behavior or forgetting how she'd been betrayed. She was simply helping a man work through something that was stopping him from healing.

With a resolute nod, she said, "I'd be happy to help you, Mr. Steele."

WADE ROLLED THE STRANGE ENDING TO HIS MEETING with Tika and Holly over and over in his mind on his drive home. He could understand Holly jumping in and reminding him that Tika didn't owe Lisa for a years-old story, but there seemed to have been more to their reaction.

Maybe he had come across as more demanding than he'd intended. He really thought that Tika would feel the same— that she owed it to Lisa to prove if she was intentionally harmed. Not because Lisa had done her some great favor by telling the world she'd faced unfair prejudice at her school, but because...

Wade blew out his breath. Okay. He had come across as too demanding. That hadn't been his intent. He was desperate for help, and he didn't know what else to do. He knew in his heart there was more to Lisa falling down the stairs. He *knew* that.

After tugging his tie loose, he pressed a button on the steering wheel to connect his phone. "Call Mom."

Within seconds of the sound of the first ring, his mother's sedate voice answered.

"Hi, Mom, just checking in," Wade said.

"We're doing okay, honey. How are you?"

He stopped himself from telling her where he'd been. Losing their only daughter was taking a hell of a toll on his parents. His mom had always been soft spoken, quiet, but she seemed broken now. He hadn't shared his suspicions with her, and he wouldn't unless they were confirmed. Lisa's death was hard enough to accept without adding another layer to the process of healing.

If, in fact, Tika proved that someone was threatening Lisa, Wade would take the evidence to the police detective he'd contacted. He would request—no, *demand*—that he officially open a case looking into Lisa's death. Until then, there was no need to upset his mom.

He told her about his day—other than the visit to HEARTS Investigative Services—and listened to her tell him about hers. Then, before the call ended, she asked the inevitable. Had he started packing up Lisa's apartment yet? They had until the end of the month to clear out her belongings. They had to get started on boxing up her things. *Correction.* Wade had to get started. He had promised his parents he'd take care of it to ease their stress.

He glanced at the car behind him to see if Tika was still tailing him. She'd offered to go with him to collect Lisa's electronic devices so she and her team could hack into them since Wade didn't have the passwords. He hoped that would be the extent of what he needed Tika to do. She hadn't seemed particularly pleased to be helping him.

Again, he thought of how oddly she and Holly had reacted to his reasons for asking her for help. There was something more there. Something he didn't know. Maybe Lisa and

Tika had a falling out that Lisa hadn't told him about. If that was the case, Tika really needed to let it go now that Lisa was gone. There was no point holding a grudge against a dead person.

He parked in the guest parking area of Lisa's apartment complex and waited for Tika to park next to him. They were quiet as they walked to the building and Wade used a fob to unlock the outer door and gestured for her to enter. The hallway always smelled musty, making Wade want to quicken his pace. He had no idea how old the carpet was, but he was certain the worn-down dark green shade hadn't been on trend since the mid-1990s. He had tried to get Lisa to move in with him until she could afford a nicer place, but she had refused. She was determined to make it on her own. Every time he tried to take care of her, she reminded him that she was the older sibling and didn't need her baby brother saving her.

"How did a lawyer end up working as a private investigator?" he asked as they walked side by side toward the elevator. Sadly, it had taken his sister's death for the building manager to finally fix the damn thing.

Tika looked up at him, her big brown eyes so filled with blatant offense he had to frown.

He couldn't seem to say anything right since he met her. "I just mean..."

"I'm not a lawyer. I dropped out of school," she told him. "I only planned on taking a break to bounce back, but I never went back."

He stopped walking, but she took three more steps before turning to look at him. She looked like an attorney. Her dark suit was pressed, her black hair was pulled into a tight bun on the back of her head. She held her shoulders back and her head high. She pulled off the confident attorney look perfectly.

"Why?" he asked. "Didn't things get better after the article?"

"No," she stated. "Where are we going?" Clearly, she was done with this conversation.

He reached around her and pressed the button to call the elevator car. "Fourth floor."

He barely got the words out before a ding filled his ears and the doors slid open. He followed her inside. The doors closed them in as he pressed the button with the worn number four. Tense silence hovered between them. He debated if he should ask in what ways things hadn't gotten better.

In truth, he didn't have to ask. As a teacher, he knew all too well how some educators viewed minority students. He did his best to take a few extra steps to connect with those kids, but by the time they reached high school, many already seemed beaten down by the unfair treatment they'd faced for so long.

"I'm sorry," he said instead.

Tika offered the slightest hint of a smile. "Thanks."

When the elevator stopped, she followed him to Lisa's door. Once inside, he flipped on the overhead light and held the door open for Tika.

In contrast to the outdated style in the hallway, Lisa's walls were a crisp white, the charcoal-and-white chevron curtains matched an area rug that lay square between her white sofa and the television attached to the wall. Her coffee table was the same white and dark-gray colors patterned in faux slate. Everything about the apartment was modern, clean, and contemporary.

Lisa had kept her apartment clean and organized, rarely leaving anything out of place. Once she was gone, things had gotten strewn about as he started sorting papers and sticky notes.

Wade had thrown out quite a bit of inconsequential things like pens and old scraps of paper, but he hadn't managed to box up a single thing. The boxes he had collected for the task were in a stack in the corner of her bedroom, but they were all still empty. He was going to have to get started on that soon.

The knowledge of that weighed on him until Tika put her hand on his arm.

"Are you okay?" she asked.

Wade nodded as he tossed his keys into the little cat-shaped dish on the table next to the door. "Yeah. Let me grab her phone and laptop for you."

He wished he'd thought to take the items with him to the HEARTS office. It would have saved Tika the trip and him the heartache of coming to Lisa's apartment. Not that he could avoid it forever.

The bag next to the couch had her laptop and phone, but the chargers were in her home office. By the time he returned with the two cords, Tika had left the front entry and walked to the bookshelf in the living room that was filled with awards and photos.

Pride filled his chest. "She was an amazing journalist."

When Tika didn't agree, he dropped the cords in the bag and moved to stand next to her.

"Did Lisa do something to upset you?" he asked.

A smirk pulled at Tika's full lips. The lipstick that had tinted her lips earlier had worn off at some point, probably from the way she constantly rubbed the tip of her pointer finger over them. That was a nervous habit, he guessed. Something she didn't realize she did. Her lips were still dark, like her skin, but naturally so instead of painted a deep berry shade.

"I guess you could say that," Tika said. "But it was a long time ago, so it doesn't really matter now."

"Is that why Holly was hesitant about you taking my case?"

She finally stopped looking at the awards and eyed him. He felt like he wanted to confess something, but he wasn't sure what.

She had a cold, hard stare. "You really don't know?"

"No."

"It doesn't matter, Mr. Steele," she said as she picked up a photo.

"Wade," he clarified. "That was my college graduation party."

"You both look very happy."

Wade smiled. "She was a great sister. She was older than me and liked to boss me around, but she was great. I miss her."

"I'm sorry." Tika sounded sincere in her condolences, even if she did have some kind of grudge against Lisa.

"Do you have any siblings?"

Tika smiled, a real smile. "Two older brothers. Both attorneys."

"Oh, that leaves you the odd man out. Odd *woman* out."

A soft smile tugged at her lips, and she tilted her head. The change in her posture made her seem less defensive. "I don't want to say my parents and brothers were disappointed. They understood, but I do think they would prefer I went back to school. I like what I do, though, and this worked out great. My brothers hire our team when they need someone investigated, and we refer them when our clients need attorneys."

"That's nice. I'm a science teacher, so there was never an opportunity for me to work with Lisa, but that would have been cool."

"It is cool." She skimmed over the shelf again. "She sure did win a lot of awards."

That sense of pride rolled through him again. "She really cared about people. She wanted to right the injustices of the world. Okay," he stated when she quirked an eyebrow. "There it is again. That subtle little sign of disbelief. Tell me what happened."

"Wade, I—"

"Did she botch the story? Attribute the wrong quote to you? What?"

"She gave them my name," Tika blurted out. "She said she wouldn't, but she did, and I got in a lot of trouble because of it."

Wade's heart dropped. Even he knew that reporters weren't supposed to reveal their sources without permission. "There must have been a misunderstanding."

"Yeah," she said flatly. "There must have been."

He gently caught her arm as she turned away from him. "There's more. Tell me."

Tika sighed. "I'm not going to speak ill of the dead. My mother taught me better than that."

"The truth isn't speaking ill," Wade said.

Silence lingered between them for several heartbeats before she conceded. "Lisa heard from one of my roommates that I had complained about a few professors who were acting in ways that made me feel discriminated against. I got lower marks for comparable work to my classmates. I was skipped over for opportunities for additional credit or work outside the classroom. Little things like that add up over time.

"She came to me and asked if she could interview me. I refused because I knew the kind of hell that would rain down on me. She promised to protect me, but at the first sign of trouble, she rolled over and gave up my name. I had to face a review board, and even though they agreed with me and fired two professors, I was blamed. They made my life hell until I left. I was planning on enrolling somewhere else, but now that I'm at HEARTS, I really don't want to go back into all that. I'm happy where I've landed."

"It was a mistake," Wade said softly. "She was young. Scared. Who knows what they told her, Tika. Who knows what kind of threats they made. But she wouldn't have just rolled over like you said. She would have pushed back. I know her. She wouldn't have sold you out unless she had to."

"Journalists have gone to jail protecting their witnesses, Wade. She didn't even get suspended."

"She was young. She didn't know better."

Tika took a breath before shrugging. "Yeah, maybe so. But she ratted me out, and I went through hell. And that's why Holly was hesitant for me to take this case. She knows I left school because of the fallout from that article. She knows how much Lisa hurt me. Even if it wasn't intentional."

"I'm sorry," he said sincerely. "And I *know* Lisa would be sorry, too. She never wanted to hurt anyone. Believe me, Tika. Look at this shelf." He thought the awards verified his sister was a good person. She was recognized over and over for shining light on the darkness, helping those who felt they couldn't help themselves. "She tried hard to make things better. She wouldn't do that now. She would be braver now."

Tika's stiff posture softened. "Yeah. We're all a little braver now than we were in college, I guess."

He smiled. "Thank you for agreeing to help me. I can see why you weren't so sure, but I promise you, Lisa never meant to cause you pain. She never would have done that on purpose."

Tika crossed the room and picked up the bag with Lisa's devices. "I'll be in touch once I can get into these."

"Thanks."

She busied herself for a while, as if nervous to ask whatever was on her mind. Finally, she looked at him. "I need to see where she fell, Wade. I need to determine if there was a hazard on the stairs that made an accident likely."

His stomach tightened. He'd managed to avoid the stairs since Lisa's death. The elevator was miraculously fixed the next day. "Uh, there's only one stairwell. At the end of the hall."

She nodded. "Okay. Thanks."

"Tika," he called as she turned toward the door. "I'm really glad I found you so I could clear the air on my sister's behalf."

She smiled, but it seemed forced, like it had earlier in the afternoon. "Me too."

He watched her leave before turning to the photo of Lisa and him at his college graduation. He didn't have to question his convictions. Lisa never would have revealed a source if she hadn't had to. Being a college student, she was probably easily intimidated. But she never would have done that now. Never.

[2]

THE NEXT MORNING, Tika eased Lisa's laptop and cell phone onto Sam's desk. "Hey, super hacker, do you have time to help me with these? Eva's out today, and I don't have that particular skillset."

Sam canted her head and twisted her bright-pink lips into a frown. Though her blond hair was pulled back, a strand had fallen free and rested against her cheek. "Depends. Is this for that backstabber who ruined your life?"

Tika wasn't surprised by Sam's snarky reaction. The women of HEARTS had a tendency to bring out their claws when one of their own was being attacked. But what Sam seemed to forget was that Lisa wasn't attacking Tika. Lisa was gone. Sam was trying to protect her from a dead woman. Though her heart was in the right place, Tika wasn't sure she appreciated the approach.

"Do you mean the woman who tragically died recently, Samantha?"

Sam didn't take the hint to chill out. She simply gave a single, but firm nod. "Yup, that's the one."

Tika scowled at her coworker. "Have some compassion, you jerk. She's only been gone a few weeks."

Lifting a perfectly arched brow, Sam said, "She gained your trust and then threw you under the bus to further her own career. I have no sympathy for someone like that."

Tika couldn't argue with Sam's assessment of Lisa's behavior. That was a pretty good summary of what had happened and what Lisa had done. Even though Tika still had plenty of residual anger to work through, she also had sympathy for Wade and his parents. They'd lost someone who had mattered to them. No matter what Lisa had done, Tika needed to try to find a way to put her personal feelings aside if she was going to help them determine what had happened to their loved one.

"That happened years ago," Tika said, more to remind herself than to inform Sam. "And she's really not in a position to do that again, so I guess we should let that go."

"If you say so." Sam dramatically grabbed Lisa's devices and pulled them closer. "What do you need?"

"Access to her emails, texts, and all those other incredibly private things you are so good at breaking into. Her brother thinks she was being threatened. I'd really love to know if she was and, if so, who was behind the threats."

Sam offered Tika a weak salute before turning her attention to the smartphone. Between Sam and Eva, there wasn't a device the HEARTS hadn't been able to break into yet. That made Tika equal parts proud and terrified. Her teammates could be downright frightening sometimes.

With Holly's Army training, Eva's police training, and Rene's time spent as a U.S. Marshal, they had the badassery fairly well covered. Alexa knew so many ins and outs of finding missing persons that Tika was certain if she ever decided to make someone disappear, they would never be found. And Sam? There didn't seem to be any secret safe from her. She could break into bank records, sealed adoptions, traffic violations, and probably a lot more that HEARTS hadn't yet found a need for.

Yeah. Her team was equally badass and terrifying. And she was thrilled to be a part of them. Once she proved herself by helping Wade, she was confident Holly would allow her to take on some of the more complex cases brought to the team.

And there was that giddy feeling again. She was so excited to be working a real investigation.

Tika had barely set her bag on her desk before Holly tapped her knuckles on the office door. This little visit arrived later than Tika had expected. She had actually anticipated a call after she'd left the office the day before. Holly had been hesitant to let Tika take Wade's case, so she had been waiting for the moment her boss would check in and make sure she was still up for helping Wade determine if foul play had a hand in Lisa's death.

"Good morning, Holly," Tika said with extra pep.

Holly scoffed. "It is too damn early for that fake reassuring smile of yours."

Tika chuckled. "Who said it's fake?"

"You're as transparent as they come, Tik." Holly crossed the small office until she was standing in front of the chair perched on the other side of Tika's desk. That chair was usually occupied by one of her teammates stopping to visit and eat candy out of the dish she kept on her desk. "How are you handling all this?"

"I'm fine," Tika said.

"You didn't come back to the office yesterday. How did things go with Wade Steele?"

She pressed her lips together and shrugged as she sat. "Okay, I guess."

Her attempt at being casual made Holly lean closer and cock her brows. Holly was good at that hard stare thing, but Rene was the master. Rene's stare could make the Hoover Dam crack. Even so, Tika had to look away as she sank back in her chair. Trying to reassure Holly without spilling the beans was pointless. Holly would just stand there and pick her apart until she told her everything that had kept her awake the night before.

"Wade asked why things got weird during the meeting," Tika explained, "so I told him how Lisa made things a million times worse for me because she wrote a scathing article and then gave up my name. He thinks she was too young and naïve to handle the pressure the school administration put on her. He swears she never would have done that if she'd had more experience."

"That sounds plausible. Do you believe him?"

Tika didn't want to sound foolish, but she did believe him. Or at least she really wanted to. "I had to face the board myself, Holly. That was easily one of the most terrifying days of my life. So, yes, I can understand how Lisa would have folded under the pressure. I can see how she got scared and felt intimidated to do what they told her. I want to believe that's why she sold me out. No. I *need* to so I can put all that mess behind me. I've blamed her for ruining my life for years. I want to let that anger go now."

"But is immersing yourself in Lisa Steele's death the best way to do that?" Holly pressed.

Holly might come across as stone cold to some, but Tika and the rest of the HEARTS understood her. She had walls ten miles thick until she opened the gate and let someone in. Once someone was in, Holly would protect them to the death. Right now, she was ready to pounce in and save Tika if need be.

Tika absolutely loved that about her. But she didn't need saving. Not this time. "You know, what? I think it is. Intentional or not, she upended my life. I've resented her for a long time. It's time for me to find a way to let that go. I think helping her family come to terms with her death will help me come to terms with the impact she had on my life. Seeing her as a person who was loved instead of as this destructive force that changed everything for me will be healing."

"She caused you a lot of pain, Tika."

"Yes, she did," she admitted. Holly knew that, but she'd never understand the depth of that pain. "But Wade made me stand back and take a look at it from a different angle. I don't think she shared my name with as much malice as I'd always thought. I think she was scared and cornered and maybe didn't know what else to do. That happens far too often to young women."

Holly tilted her head so far, her straight blond hair fell from her shoulder as she stared Tika down with her ice-blue eyes. She was trying to determine if Tika was being honest with herself. If there was a hint of doubt in her defense, Holly would see it. Tika didn't even blink.

"Okay," Holly said. "But if you decide you can't work this case, you just say the word and I'll take over. I won't think less of you. You're a great investigator. I know that."

If Holly were the type to hug, Tika would have jumped up and given her a huge embrace. Instead, she smiled. "Thank you for that. I appreciate it. Listen, Holly, at the end of the day, it doesn't matter what my past is with Lisa. This isn't even about her, not really. At the core, this is about her brother. He's hurting right now. If I can help him, I should. That's why we're here, right?"

"That is why we're here. But that doesn't mean *you* have to help him. Any one of us can look through Lisa's files and see if there was a viable threat made against her. It does *not* have to be you."

Tika smiled. "I know and I appreciate that. If it gets to be too personal, I'll ask you to assign someone else. For now, though, I think this will help me find closure on a few things."

Holly straightened her posture as she frowned. "One more thing. If he crosses a line—"

Tika didn't mean to let her amusement at the warning slip, but a little giggle left her. "I don't think that's an issue, Holly."

Holly didn't laugh. She didn't even smile. "I do. I saw how he was looking at you yesterday. He's grieving, and he feels connected to you because of your past with his sister. I'm not saying he will act inappropriately, but if he does..."

"I know how to take care of myself, Holly," Tika stated firmly. "You've taught me well, *Sensei*."

And she had. Tika had never taken a self-defense class in her life, but thanks to her team members, she was as capable as someone who had earned several belts in martial arts, or so they'd told her. She'd also learned how to shoot a gun. Eva had promised to teach her how to throw knives, but those lessons hadn't started yet. Tika wasn't going to let her forget, though. Knife throwing was *definitely* something she wanted to learn.

Holly lifted a brow at Tika's sarcasm, but then bowed slightly and disappeared.

After flipping open her laptop, Tika rubbed her hands together while it powered up. "Okay," she whispered. "Let's get this party started."

She had spent some time the evening before researching Lisa's career. Wade hadn't been joking about the work she'd done. She had used her journalism degree to tackle big issues for the little guy. From corporations overworking their minimum-wage employees to sexism to other abuses of power, Lisa really seemed to have tried to do good.

Tika had to admire her for that. Despite the missteps Lisa had taken in handling Tika's story, she seemed to have found her way and focused on serving the underdogs of the world.

Just a few years ago, Lisa had sat in a café off campus and begged Tika to talk to her. Tika had been furious that her sorority sister had betrayed her confidence. She never would have said a word if she'd known her roommate would betray her—and to the school paper no less!

Lisa had been relentless in her promises and reassurances. Under no circumstances would she reveal Tika's name. *Ever.* That had been the agreement. Right up until Tika got pulled into the dean's office and asked about the story that had been published. She had tried to deny that she was Lisa's source, but after her third attempt, the dean had told her that Lisa had given her up. Lisa had rolled over. Lisa had exposed Tika and all her secrets.

The months that followed had been the worst of Tika's life. Her parents threatened to sue if the administration didn't stop harassing Tika and forcing her to miss classes to answer questions, but that wasn't even the worst of what she had been through. The worst was when her so-called friends—the people who had vowed to forever and always be there for her —pushed her away.

She found herself standing alone in her fight, and she quickly decided it wasn't a fight worth having.

Lisa graduated soon after her article exposed the prevalence of racism on campus and left Tika vulnerable to retaliation. Tika had another year of her undergraduate degree to go, and she couldn't handle it. Yes, she could have transferred, but by the time she had decided to stop fighting back, she was so disheartened, she simply needed a break.

With a shake of her head, Tika reminded herself to stop looking back. Her life was full now. She had found real friendships with her new team. The women of HEARTS would never abandon her in her time of need. These people would literally put their lives on the line to protect her. The sense of respect and belonging that she'd never found during college was in abundance at HEARTS. She would never have found her way here if life had turned out like she'd planned.

Things had a way of working out, and she was going to take this opportunity to put the past to rest. Helping Wade determine if there was more to his sister's death was her chance to face what had happened with Lisa and resolve the lingering bitterness she'd been harboring for so long.

Actually, Tika was looking forward to letting this go.

After she had left Lisa's apartment the previous day, she'd gone home and compiled a list of links to every article attributed to Lisa for the last six weeks. If someone had attacked Lisa, the anger was likely to be recent, something someone was still feeling passionate about.

The problem with that theory was Lisa seemed to only take on big issues that people felt passionate about. The most-tame stories she'd covered in the weeks leading to her death were in-depth looks at a few local politicians. The upcoming election was heated, mostly because of the political divide. There were no topics that were on fire locally, but the overall political mood was precarious, like a stick of dynamite just waiting to be lit.

Lisa had done an interview with several local politicians, but nothing about that stood out to Tika. Lawrence Butler and his wife, Karen, seemed to be the all-American couple reaching for the stars. Fake smiles, fake promises, and mile-high ambitions. William Stokes had years of experience as an elected official that he was counting on to beat Lawrence Butler. And Tabitha Benson seemed to think that it was time for women to overthrow Washington D.C.

Overall, Lisa's stories were neutral, unbiased. Nothing there made Tika think any of the candidates would be upset about the series.

The next story seemed far more promising. Clicking on the headline implying a local company was abusing their employees, she skimmed the story that Lisa had written. A stunning photo of a young woman holding up a picture caught Tika's eye, but not because the cutline explained that the woman was showing proof of the intolerable work conditions she had claimed, but because the photo was attributed to Lisa Steele.

Lisa wrote amazing and poignant stories, *and* she took incredibly creative photos that had a way of telling a story all on their own.

Tika sat back as a thought occurred to her. If Lisa took her own photos, she would have had a decent camera. The camera on a phone wouldn't produce the quality of the photos in the article Tika had just skimmed.

Grabbing the notepad on her desk, Tika jotted down a reminder to ask Wade if she could review Lisa's camera. Maybe the threats had come from someone whose story hadn't yet been published. Someone who didn't want their story to find its way into print.

With that in mind, Tika returned to reviewing Lisa's newest publications and started making a list of people who could potentially be angry at the information revealed about them. Based on the topics of the articles attributed to Lisa Steele, Tika expected the list to be very long.

WADE OPENED THE MAIN ENTRANCE OF LISA'S apartment building and smiled at Tika as she walked in with the same laptop bag she'd left with the day before. "You cracked her passwords way faster than I expected," he said.

"With the right software, hacking is actually fairly easy. I have new passwords, but we never determined if I'd go through her accounts or if you'd rather do that. I didn't want to overstep, so I haven't opened anything yet."

His chest suddenly felt tight. He hadn't considered that he might be the one to find the emails. While he wanted to find whoever was responsible—and was certain someone was—the idea of seeing the threats made against her suddenly terrified him.

Wade opened his mouth, but no words came out. What could he possibly say?

Tika seemed to sense his struggle. "Tell you what, let's set this aside for a few minutes. We don't have to dig into this right now. It'll keep. I want to ask you a few questions about Lisa's work. We can start there."

Wade took the bag from her and hefted it over his shoulder as he led her toward the elevator. "Sorry. I guess I hadn't really thought about what the next step would be."

"That's okay."

"Did you... Did anything stand out to you in the stairwell?"

"No. There are new no-slip skids on the stairs. I'm sure the building owner made sure that was done as soon as the police cleared the..." She snapped her lips closed.

"The scene," Wade finished for her. "It's okay."

"I didn't mean to sound so clinical about it."

He gave her a reassuring smile. "You don't have to tiptoe around me. I understand."

They were quiet as they rode up to the fourth floor. Once inside Lisa's apartment, Tika scanned the living room for a few seconds before her dark eyes landed on his. "You said to meet you here because you were going to be packing up Lisa's belongings."

He looked around as well. Nothing was out of place. He had moved from wall to wall and room to room, but he hadn't touched a thing. An unexpected but now familiar pain hit him. The realization that his sister was gone forever was something akin to a dull sword cutting him open from the inside out.

After swallowing hard, Wade cleared his throat and blinked rapidly for several seconds. "I was planning to, but... Lisa had a lot of shit." He turned his eyes to Tika and managed a slight smile.

"Don't we all?" she asked lightly in return.

"I told my parents I'd take care of this, but...I don't know where to start," he confessed. However, he didn't think his confession was necessarily about the packing. His sister was gone. She'd never come back. She'd never sit on that couch with a glass of wine, laughing as they reminisced about their childhood. Never again would she scoff about the bad decisions of the school board and tell Wade he was too damn good for them anyway. She'd never again tell him that being a teacher in today's world was far more noble than any other profession she could think of. He wasn't sure teaching kids chemistry was noble. Most of them simply wanted to learn how to blow things up.

"She—" He cleared his throat when his voice cracked. "I know she made mistakes with your story, but she was a good sister."

"I believe that," Tika whispered.

"This is really hard," he said. "I used to come over at least twice a month with takeout, and we'd sit there"—he gestured toward the couch—"and talk about everything. I don't know if a lot of siblings do that after they grow up, but we always did. We always talked to each other. It probably sounds trite, but she was my best friend. She really was."

Tika put her hand on his arm, squeezing lightly. "Let's take a few moments, okay?"

She was kind enough to turn her back, as if interested in the knickknacks that Lisa had collected over the years. In the meantime, Wade wiped his eyes, sniffed a few times, and dragged his hands over his hair—all in a vain attempt at pulling himself together.

After a few moments, Tika pointed at a little statuette. "Tell me about this."

He stared at the odd little shape of a genderless body holding a star over its head. "That was a gift from a sculptor she interviewed. There's still a lot of sexism in the art world. Lisa interviewed several women who had faced various types of harassment trying to secure gallery showings." He offered her a halfhearted smile. "One of them made this for Lisa. I guess the star is a representation of her voice finally being heard. Or something like that. Lisa would remember."

Tika picked up the four-inch-tall piece of clay and held it out to him. He hesitated before taking it. Once he did, she handed a square of tissue paper from the pile on the end table. Wade stared at the little figure before wrapping it up and setting it inside one of the boxes he'd brought in from the bedroom.

She selected a glass horse next. "And this one?"

Piece by piece, Tika helped him pack the contents sitting on one of Lisa's shelves. Story by story, he tucked his sister's belongings carefully away and managed to smile, even laugh, as he did so. He wouldn't have thought that was possible, but as he taped shut the first of what would be many boxes of his sister's life, warmth settled over him. He didn't feel like this was the process of accepting her death. He felt like this was the first step of a very long healing process.

"Thank you," he said softly. He set the packing tape aside and heaved a long sigh. "Sincerely. I appreciate your help."

"You're welcome."

"I know you didn't come here for this, but I appreciate that you helped get me over that first hump. I really was at a loss for how to get started."

She tilted her head, and her crown of hair shifted, catching his eye. The day before, she'd had the dark strands pulled back into a bun. Now, black coils surrounded her face like a halo. He liked this look better. She seemed softer with her hair loose. Her heart-shaped face wasn't quite as sharp around the edges.

Of course, she could appear softer because she wasn't staring at him with wide eyes as she held herself in a rigid posture as the shock of what he'd told her set in. He had spent a lot of the night rolling over what Tika had told him in his mind.

He was even more convinced today than he'd been the day before that Lisa's error in judgment had a huge impact on her decision to reveal Tika's name.

"Lisa had always been willing to stand up for people," he said without prompting, "but after college, that fire in her had seemed to be insatiable. My parents had always chalked that up to her being ambitious, but now that I know what happened with your story, I have to think that she was motivated by guilt. She must have known about the troubles her story caused you. She must have felt responsible. I think that was what pushed her all these years. That was what had motivated her to uncover corruption and wrongdoing. She couldn't make things right for you, Tika, but I think she was doing what she could to make up for her mistake. I really do."

She gave him a slight nod. "I hope you're right. I hope she took what she learned and used it to make better choices."

"She was a good person." He hated that he felt the need to keep saying that, but he did. He didn't want Tika to think poorly of his sister. For some reason, that was important to him.

"Are you ready to deal with why I am here?" Tika asked.

Wade lowered his face. "I guess I have to be, right?"

"No," she stated. "You don't have to be. If you don't want to sort through her documents and emails, I can do that for you. I know what I'm looking for. Nothing else matters to me. I'm not going to be snooping for dirt on Lisa or anyone else. I just want to help you find the information you need."

He blew out a long breath. "Yeah. I think it's best if you do that. Do you mind doing it here, though? I'd like to see anything you find."

She hesitated before saying, "Wade, I don't know how long this will take. I haven't looked at her accounts yet, so I have no idea what I'm getting into. She could have thousands of messages for me to sort through. I mean...I can stay for a while, but if I don't find anything right away, I'm going to have to take these with me and get back to you."

Heat warmed his cheeks, and he hoped he wasn't blushing. He hadn't thought about that. Or about the fact that he really just didn't want her to leave and that was his excuse. He'd blurted that request without thinking it through.

"Right. I get it. Um, yeah, if you need to go, then just...call me with an update."

She didn't move. "I can stay. For a little while." She looked at the many shelves that still needed to be packed. "If you want."

He followed her gaze, and he realized that he did want her to stay. Because having her there somehow gave him the strength to move beyond his grief and start doing what he had to do.

"I can order in pizza or something," he said.

She nodded. "Sounds good. Um, do you mind if I look through her camera, too? She might have photos on there of what she was working on."

Like a flash of lightning, he realized he hadn't seen her camera. That thing had been one of her most prized possessions. Her investment had far exceeded her budget because she knew that part of her storytelling was amazing photos. She had saved for months and spent hours scouring over her options before finally purchasing a new camera a few months ago. Even then, she had only made a choice because the strap on her old bag broke and, despite the padding, the lens of her camera cracked.

Wade slowly spun around as he searched the living room, trying to recall where he'd last seen the black camera bag.

When he'd last seen the camera bag. It wasn't tucked under the coffee table, where he'd seen it many times before, so he checked the desk in the corner of the living room. Then he went into the bedroom and peered under the bed and then poked his head in the closet.

He turned to where Tika had followed him. "It's not here."

"Could it be in her car?"

He swallowed hard. "No. No. She treated that camera better than most people treat their pets. She wouldn't leave it in her car in the dead of winter." He raked his hand through his hair. "It's missing. Her camera is missing."

Tika lifted her hands to him as if sensing his panic and seeing where his mind was going even as it traveled down the road of suspicion. "We have to eliminate all possibilities before we can assume it was taken. Go check her car, please. I'm going to look around the apartment some more."

He took Lisa's keys from the bowl next to the door and trotted to the elevator. He would have taken the stairs instead of waiting for the elevator to slowly rise to the fourth floor, but he couldn't bring himself to even enter the stairwell. His sister had fallen there. Instead, he tapped his toe as he impatiently waited.

Within minutes, the elevator carried him to the first floor, and he jogged down the hallway and out to Lisa's car. Only then did he realize he hadn't grabbed a jacket on his way out. He ignored the cold air enveloping him as he used the remote to unlock her old sedan. He searched the baseboard of the passenger seat, opened the glove box even though he knew the camera wouldn't fit there, and then he checked the back seat. Nothing. The trunk was empty except for her spare tire and the reusable grocery bags she told him she never remembered to take into the store with her.

He patted the bags to be certain, but there was nothing inside them. The camera wasn't there either.

Empty handed, Wade ran back into the warmth of the building and again impatiently awaited the elevator. He hoped Tika had found it, but when he walked into Lisa's apartment, she was bent over to look under the sofa. She sat back and shook her head.

"Maybe it needed repairs. Or someone borrowed it," she suggested.

Wade sank onto the sofa where Tika had just checked. "You don't understand how important that camera was to her," he said softly. "If it were broken, she would have told me. She would have been devastated. And she never would have loaned it out. It's gone."

She put her hand on his. "We'll find it, Wade."

He wished he could believe her, but at the moment, he was too busy kicking himself for not realizing the camera was missing sooner.

[3]

TIKA HELD up a flyer for Wade to see the moment he opened the door to Lisa's apartment building. The page had an image of the type of camera Lisa owned, the serial number and product details, and a hefty reward for its return.

"These are at every pawnshop and secondhand store within seventy-five miles," she explained. "If anyone comes in with Lisa's camera, I'll get a call."

"Thank you," he said, letting her in.

As they rode up to the fourth floor, Tika took a moment to absorb his appearance. Though he forced a smile, his eyes were bloodshot. He had a hint of five o'clock shadow, and his shoulders seemed too heavy for him to bear. He slouched, just a bit, as if carrying the weight of the world. She supposed, in a sense, he was.

As the elevator jerked to a stop, Wade told her that he had called all of Lisa's friends that he knew, and none of them had her camera. He said, once again, how much she had valued that camera and never would have loaned it to someone.

"We have to check," Tika told him. "No stone left unturned and all that."

He gave her a bashful smile. "I know. I'm sorry."

"Don't be," she said, following him from the elevator into the musty hallway. "I understand. I really do."

He unlocked Lisa's apartment and let her in. Tika stopped just a few steps inside as she noticed the bookshelves that were now bare. When she'd left him there the night before, the shelves were still filled with trinkets and framed photographs. No wonder he looked so exhausted this afternoon. He must have been up late packing away his sister's belongings.

Turning, she showed him the surprise on her face. "Wow. You made a lot of progress last night."

"I did, thanks to you. It took a while, but taking a moment to remember each piece before packing it away made it easier. Thank you for showing me that process."

His choice of words made her smile. He sounded exactly how she imagined a science teacher would in the classroom. She could easily picture him getting excited about chemistry and other nerdy science things. She'd never been good at science. English and history had been her specialties in high school.

"That's kind of a tradition in our family when we are dealing with a loss," she said as she shrugged out of her coat. "Although, the Browns tend to have wine available to ease the strain. I'm not sure if that's the strain of packing up a loved one's belongings or of us all being around each other for an extended amount of time."

He laughed as she hung her coat on the hooks by the door, and she was glad she was able to ease some of the shadows in his eyes.

"I'm just kidding," she insisted. "My family is great."

"Mine too," he said as his face softened. "I could get someone else in the family to do this, but I really feel like it should be me. I think Lisa would have wanted it to be me."

Tika put her hand to his arm in a supportive but not too personal gesture. "I'm truly sorry for all that you're going through. I'm glad I was able to help you find a starting point. Are you ready to take the next step?"

"The next step being?"

"You hired me to find out if the threats against Lisa were worth the police investigating. We got sidetracked last night, but I'm ready now. Are you?"

Wade blew out his breath. "I guess I have to be. I can't keep distracting you forever, can I?"

"No, you can't." She went to the couch where they'd left Lisa's laptop and phone the night before. While the computer booted up, she watched Wade stack a few boxes in the corner. As soon as the login screen appeared, she typed in the new information Sam had set up to give her access. "I'm in," she announced.

"You, uh... Do your thing," Wade said. "I'll be in the other room if you need me for anything. I've managed to find a groove with packing. I don't want to lose it."

Tika didn't argue. She suspected he would be hovering around her before long. If he hadn't been interested in the search, he would have allowed her to do it at her office. It was obvious to her that as much as he wanted to be tackling these things for his sister, he wasn't emotionally ready to face her death. Taking the lead on the search, letting him come around in his own time, was the least Tika could do for him.

She had just opened one of Lisa's email accounts when music filtered to her from the bedroom. Tilting her head, she listened for a few moments before identifying the beat as an old Nirvana song. She didn't have to try too hard to picture a much younger version of Wade trying to pull off the Seattle grunge look that was on trend in the late '90s.

To her surprise, she thought he probably would have looked cute with long shaggy hair, shredded jeans, and a baggy flannel shirt over a band T-shirt. The image made her laugh. That was quite different from the clean-cut science teacher he had grown up to be.

"Are you laughing at my taste in music?"

She turned on the couch enough to see him standing behind her with his hands on his hips and his eyes narrowed suspiciously. If he had been able to hide his smirk, she might have been concerned he was really upset. The slight tilt to his lips and hint of a dimple in his left cheek gave him away. She loved that, despite his obvious weariness, he was able to have a moment of lightheartedness.

"Just a little bit," she said.

"Let me guess. You were one of those Celine Dion fan girls."

"Lord no," she stated with a firm shake of her head, but then shrugged. "Okay. I might know all the words to every song she ever sang, but that doesn't mean I was a fan girl."

"I got you," he said and disappeared.

Moments later, the theme song from *Titanic* filled the apartment.

"Better?" Wade called from the bedroom.

"Much," she responded and focused on the computer again. Her concentration was broken, however, when Wade started singing out of tune and slightly off beat. She couldn't say for certain, but she was pretty sure his horrible rendition of a beautiful song was intentional.

"Little man," Tika muttered, "you need to stop. This was a good song until you came along." She couldn't stop herself from smiling. Yeah, he was definitely putting on a show for her, teasing her in his own way. Halfway through the second verse, though, she had all she could handle.

"Wade!"

"Yeah?"

"Put the grunge music back on. You're ruining the best part of my childhood right now."

"That's cruel, Tika," he answered.

"So is your singing," she whispered and then laughed at her joke as Celine Dion was cut short. Seconds later, Nirvana was back on, and she immediately regretted her request.

Tika didn't really have a plan of attack to get through Lisa's emails, she just knew the email account was where she intended to start her search. Wade had told her that Lisa had been upset about threats the night they'd had dinner, days before her death. She verified the date that Lisa had written in her notes and started there, working backward in the inbox.

"Oh," she said under her breath when she came across an email titled *Fuck Off.* "Well, that's interesting." She opened the email from someone named Erin Diaz. The email was dated two days before Lisa's fall. Skimming over the scathing contents, Tika got the gist of it. Erin insisted that Lisa's lame attempts at apologizing were not nearly enough to make amends for what she'd done, and if she sent flowers one more time, Erin was going to shove them...

"*Okay*, we have a starting point," Tika said after she read the descriptive terms that Erin used to explain what she planned to do with the next delivery. Pushing herself up, she walked to the bedroom but stopped in the doorway and leaned against the wooden jamb. She stood there unnoticed, listening to Wade butchering an already terrible song. "Did you have a girlfriend in high school?" she asked.

He quit bouncing his head and singing to look at her. "Once."

"Just once?"

That already familiar hint of a teasing smile curved his lips. "For like three days."

"Did she hear you sing?"

He laughed. "No, but she saw me dance." He demonstrated by doing a terrible display of moonwalking across the small, carpeted bedroom.

Tika dramatically sighed at him and then headed toward the pile of clothes he had been folding. "Does the name Erin Diaz mean anything to you?"

Wade's face fell. "She's Lisa's ex. They broke up about two months ago. Why?"

"Do you know why they broke up?"

"No. Lisa never wanted to talk about it, but they didn't date very long. Not even a year. Why?" he asked again.

Tika picked up a pink blouse and started folding it. "She sent a not-so-pleasant email to Lisa. Not a threat," she quickly clarified. "At least not one to be taken seriously, but I'd like to talk to her. She might know more about what Lisa was working on in the last few months or who might have been making threats against her." She added the shirt to the pile he'd been putting together to pack. "Do you mind if I contact her?"

He shook his head. "I want you to do whatever you need to do to find out what happened to Lisa."

Tika bit at her lip as she ran her fingers over a few pearl buttons on a blouse in the pile he'd taken from the closet. "You do understand that this may have simply been an accident, right? We may never find proof that someone hurt her." She lifted her eyes to his, not only to make sure he was hearing her but to gauge his response. "You know that, don't you?"

He hesitated before nodding. "Yeah, I know that. But if someone did this to her, I want to know who and why."

"Okay. I will reach out to Erin and keep looking for other information. You keep practicing those dance moves. Maybe you'll get it someday."

"These moves?" he asked as he started twisting his hips and shaking his butt.

"You need help," she said.

In response to her suggestion, Wade started exaggerating how bad his dancing was.

She laughed and left him to finish packing up Lisa's clothes. After unlocking Lisa's phone, Tika scrolled the contacts until she found information for Erin Diaz. Typing the number into her phone, Tika cleared her throat and rolled her shoulders back. She had learned along the way that standing tall and confident helped her project herself better, even on a phone call. Little tricks like that helped her psych herself up for these moments when she was feeling nervous.

She couldn't really pinpoint why she felt nervous, though. Calling and requesting information was something she was incredibly familiar with at this point, but something in the pit of her stomach tightened, causing a flash of anxiety. She had a sense, somewhere deep inside, that Wade was going to regret digging into Lisa's personal life.

He clearly held his sister in high regard. Tika's experiences may have been long ago, and though she was determined to forgive and forget, part of her still clung to the hurt of Lisa's betrayal. She didn't want to expose Wade to any more of that than she already had by coming clean about her experience with his sister.

Tika listened to the first ring, then the second. Erin answered on the third.

"Ms. Diaz," Tika said, "my name is Tika Brown. I'm a private investigator with HEARTS Investigative Services. I've been hired by Lisa Steele's family to look into her death. May I ask you a few questions?"

There was a long pause. That wasn't unusual. Many people were taken aback by the idea of a PI calling to question them.

"I don't know anything about her death."

Tika assured her by saying, "I'm not implying that you do, but I think you can help me sort through a few things if you have a moment."

"I don't—"

"Why did you and Lisa break up?" she asked, cutting off Erin's attempt at getting out of the conversation. Alexa had taught her that trick. Pushing buttons got a reaction that was more likely to be honest. Sometimes keeping people off balance kept them from coming up with an alternative story.

"That's personal."

"It must have been a bad break up. I read the emails you sent. You weren't very open to her attempts at making amends."

A loud sigh echoed through the phone. "Ms. Brown was it?"

"Yes."

"I told Lisa nicely multiple times that I wasn't ready to forgive her. She chose to continue to push the issue. So I sent a rather harsh email to make myself even more clear. I was angry, not homicidal. I'm sure you've had to do that with persistent exes before. I'm fairly sure everyone has at least once. That doesn't mean I actually wished her harm."

"Again, I'm not implying that."

"What *are* you implying?"

"Nothing, actually. I'm just hoping you can answer a few questions for me." Tika turned and looked toward the bedroom.

Wade was watching her. The stress had returned to his eyes. He had managed a few minutes of lightheartedness. Tika hated that she'd put an end to that by asking about Erin. He stood, with a light-blue piece of material in his hands, waiting.

"Lisa told her brother she had been receiving threats. Had she ever shared that with you?"

Erin scoffed. "Lisa was an investigative reporter who made it her business to destroy people. She got threats all the time."

"Do you know who or what she was investigating when you broke up?"

"Um, some politician. Lawrence Butler, I think."

Tika stood even taller. She had seen an article about the Butlers and their rise to Midwestern political power. They had their sights set on Washington D.C. next, and Lisa's article seemed to imply they had what it took to get there.

"She didn't buy his down-home country charms," Erin continued. "She thought he was hiding something and planned to dig deeper into his past."

"Did she ever say what she thought he was hiding?"

"No. I never knew much about her work until it was published, Ms. Brown. She tried to protect me from worrying, so she didn't talk to me about her job. I wish I'd done the same."

Tika tilted her head. "What do you—"

"I have to go. I'm not going to lose another job because of her."

Pulling the phone from her ear, Tika verified that the call had ended. "Well. She confirmed that Lisa received threats, but she wasn't clear on what they were or how they were made. Or at least she didn't want to tell me about them."

"Maybe she thought you were looking into her," Wade suggested.

"Maybe. Do you know where she works? I'll see if she'll be more open to talking face-to-face."

Wade creased his brow for a few seconds before shaking his head. "No. Not anymore. She worked for the city as a paralegal for a while, but she—"

"Lost her job?"

"Yeah. Right before she and Lisa broke up. How did you know?"

"It sounds like she blames Lisa for that. Any idea why?"

Wade turned and tossed the shirt he'd been holding into the bedroom before crossing the room to stand in front of Tika. "No. I don't. I just know that their breakup was ugly and Lisa took it hard. She felt bad about it."

"Could that be because she did something that got Erin in trouble?"

He shook his head. "I don't know how she could. Besides, she wouldn't have done anything to hurt Erin. She loved her. She told me she was thinking about asking Erin to move in with her a few weeks before things ended between them."

"But she never told you why things ended?"

He looked bewildered. "No."

Tika eased onto the couch and gestured for him to sit next to her. "How well did you know Erin?"

"She was around quite a bit when they were dating, but I can't say that I knew her well," he said, sinking onto the other side of the couch. "We had dinner several times. She came to my parents' anniversary party last year. Lisa tended to keep her relationships private. Not just who she was dating but her friendships as well. She was always like that."

"Do you think Erin would talk to you? She may feel

intimidated by me because I'm an investigator. But you're Lisa's brother, someone she knew. She might be more open to coming clean to you."

"I should go see her." He focused on Tika, but she could still see lingering confusion in his eyes.

"That's probably the best bet to get her to open up," Tika agreed. "But are you okay with that?"

His frown indicated he wasn't, but he nodded and ran his hands over his thighs. "What do you need to know?"

"I'd like to know why they broke up and if she had any idea who might have threatened Lisa. How they threatened her. If we can narrow it down to email, social media, or phone calls, I can get through this much faster."

Wade looked at his watch. "I don't know where she works now, but I'd bet she still runs along the same path every day. Tomorrow is Saturday. I bet we can catch her at the park."

"I don't know that she'll be very open if I'm there with you."

"Maybe not, but I can't do a stakeout alone. Well, I could, but...I don't want to."

A little spark of excitement lit in Tika's stomach. Sitting in a car watching people go by, waiting for one person in particular, wasn't the most exciting part of being a private investigator, but she still loved that part of her job.

"Okay. I'll go with you," she said. "On one condition."

"What's that?"

"I get to pick the music."

WADE WASN'T MUCH OF A COFFEE DRINKER, BUT HE HAD stayed up half the night trying to think of anything that Lisa might have said about Erin. Anything that might have indicated why they split. He had barely crawled from his bed when Tika texted that she was outside his building, waiting for him. She'd brought him coffee and though that wasn't his favorite beverage, he had sipped it as Tika drove to the park where Wade thought they might find Erin.

He couldn't help but think that the mid-1990s-era pop music was his punishment for intentionally tormenting her with his singing the day before. It was worth the price he was paying, though. He had needed the teasing to ease his stress. For some reason, Tika seemed to be the one thing that made the void in his life a little easier to take.

Tika pulled into the parking lot at the area park where a lot of joggers parked because a sidewalk led to the path. "There," he said and gestured toward a silver SUV. "I'm pretty sure that's Erin's."

Tika slowed down as she drove by the vehicle, and Wade read the license plate. *EDIAZ2*.

"Yup," he said. "That's hers."

Tika backed her sedan into a spot in the row behind the SUV so they could keep an eye out for Erin. She left the car running but turned down the heat. He was tempted to thank her. He'd been sweating ever since she picked him up. Her car was like a freaking sauna. He'd kept his complaint to himself since she hadn't seemed to mind the heat.

As they waited, she pulled the top off her cup. "Did you happen to read Lisa's article on Lawrence and Karen Butler?"

The question might have sounded casual, but Wade was

quickly learning that Tika's "casual" conversation tended to be deeper than most. She wasn't asking about the article. She was trying to find out if there was more to it than what was on the surface.

Wade watched two women head toward the running path. "Why do people do this to themselves?" he asked. "It's freezing out there."

"Are you averting my question or just easily distracted?" Tika asked.

"Both." He grinned as he looked at her. "I was dissecting your question, actually. Why are you asking about that? That was months ago."

"I didn't think much about it initially, but there was an entire folder in her email inbox dedicated to them."

Wade turned his attention from Erin's car to the woman sitting behind the steering wheel. She had a bright-blue knit cap pulled down over her ears. The hat and her mittens must have been a set since they were perfectly matched. The color reminded him of clear sunny spring days. For some reason, he thought that was an odd color choice for winter items, but he liked the way the light color stood out against her skin.

Her hair seemed to be different every time he saw her. This time, she'd used a curling iron or some other device to make waves. Her hair was longer in this style, going well beyond her shoulders. He thought he liked this look almost as much as he liked the coils she'd been sporting the day before.

He must have stared for too long, because she lifted her brows at him and dipped her chin a bit.

"If you know something about Lawrence Butler, you damn well better spit it out," she warned.

Wade smiled, and then he chuckled and forced his attention back to the SUV. "Sorry. I was... I like your hat."

"My hat?"

"It's a nice color on you," he added before sipping his drink.

She seemed hesitant in saying, "Thank you."

Awkward silence surrounded them as he debated if he should try to explain his stupid hat comment. But she broke through the weirdness.

"What do you know about Lawrence Butler?" she asked.

He shrugged. "Not much. I just know that Lisa didn't buy the act he and his wife put on for her. I guess they were very stiff around each other, making her suspect there were problems in their marriage. She said they were common clothes moths pretending to be monarch butterflies and hoping no one noticed. I remember that because it made me laugh," he said as a rush of sentimentality hit him. "She had a strange way of describing people sometimes."

"Erin mentioned them on the phone yesterday. She thought the same thing—that Lisa was suspicious of their behavior. I looked into her email a bit more and found that she had been asking people for interviews about Butler after the original article was posted. I haven't found any of these so-called threats, though. Do you know if she used a cloud drive? She hadn't added one to her favorite links, but that doesn't mean anything."

"I'm sure she must have," he said. "She wouldn't have kept all that valuable information on a laptop that could crash or get stolen. She would have uploaded backups somewhere, but I don't know which one she was using. I'll take some time to look through her files this afternoon if you want to focus on something else. We can grab some lunch and head over to her apartment after I talk to Erin."

Wade leaned forward when he saw a jogger wearing weather-resistant running pants and a bright-pink hoodie headed down the sidewalk toward the parking lot. As she neared, with her dark-brown ponytail bouncing behind her, he released his seatbelt.

"There she is," he said.

"Be cool," Tika suggested as he climbed from her car.

Wade stuffed his hands in his pockets, suddenly uneasy about facing Erin, and headed for her SUV. She slowed her stride when she spotted him, looking suspicious as he stopped by her vehicle. He knew the moment she recognized him by the way her posture softened.

"Hey," she said, her voice still breathless from her round of exercise.

"Hi," Wade said, reminded of what Tika had said. *Be cool.* "I'm sorry to bother you like this. I didn't know how else to find you."

"It's okay." She fussed with digging in her hoodie pocket as she continued to pant and then focused on using the remote start on her key fob to turn on the engine of her SUV. Several seconds passed before she met his eyes. "I'm sorry about Lisa. I really am, Wade. I know how close you two were."

"Thank you."

"If this is about the email I sent, I told that PI that was done in anger—"

"I know you didn't hurt Lisa," he said before she could

finish. "I never thought you did. I just need to know if you have any idea who might have."

A little puff of mist left her as she huffed. "I was told that she fell."

"She did, but I think there was more to it. I think someone was after her. She told me she'd been threatened."

She looked at him with sad hazel eyes. "Wade, nothing good can come from you digging into Lisa's rivalries. Let this go, okay."

Her answer actually made him more determined to do the opposite. "What rivalries?"

"Basically everyone she ever talked to, Wade. She made enemies like most people make cookies. By the *dozens*."

His heart started to beat faster. "Like who?"

She frowned at him. "Let it go."

"I can't. My sister is dead, Erin. I have reason to believe someone caused her fall, but I don't know who that could be. If you have any idea—"

"It could be anyone. I know you have this idealistic vision of her because she was your big sister, but Lisa was a manipulative bitch who would have thrown you, your mother, your fucking dog, under the bus to get ahead. She double crossed anyone who got between her and a story without thinking twice about it."

He felt like a knife went through him. That's pretty much how Tika had viewed Lisa, too. But Tika had been wrong. So was Erin. "No. She wouldn't—"

"She got me fired because a story was more important to her than I was," Erin stated as she furrowed her brow. The hard tone of her voice made it clear the anger she felt was still raw. "She'd pour me a glass of wine, rub my shoulders, and get me to tell her about my day. Whenever I'd hesitate, she'd remind me that she knew how important confidentiality was. She'd tell me how I could trust her. And I did, but the first time I shared something she could use to write a story, she didn't hesitate."

"I'm sure she didn't mean for you to get fired," Wade said.

"Well, I'm glad that you're sure, because I'm not. A journalist dating a member of the city paralegal team got her hands on confidential information. How long do you think it took them to trace that back to me? Two days," she stated before he could reply. "I was fired within two days of her little exposé hitting the newspaper. I lost my job because my girlfriend used our private conversation as a source to write a story. She didn't even warn me, Wade. She didn't even ask. She just did what she did, which was use people to get what she wanted." She shook her head as she calmed down. "I'm sorry, but it's the truth. She manipulated everyone into trusting her, into talking to her, but she never hesitated in violating that trust if it benefited her."

"You're wrong about her," he said, but his voice didn't hold the conviction he thought it should have.

"Wade," she said so softly he barely heard her, "if you're looking for someone who would want to hurt Lisa, the list is incredibly long. I'm sorry, but you really should let this go so you don't lose this version of her that you love so much."

"Someone threatened her," he said. "Now she's dead. I can't let that go."

Erin looked around the park before sighing heavily. "Start with a man named Dylan Tyler. She named him in some story she wrote in college. She accused him of being a racist, and it sounds like that accusation is still following him."

Wade swallowed hard. That must have been the same article Tika had been so upset about.

"Lisa told me he blames her for having trouble finding decent work even though that article was in a college paper years ago," Erin continued. "Search engines have a way of making sure no one ever outgrows their past. I don't know how serious his threats were, but she told me a few months ago that he threatened to make her pay for what she'd done to him."

"Did she say if that was in an email or a phone call?"

"I don't know, but her byline always had her email included, so I would think that's the best place to start."

Wade nodded. "I'll look into that. Thank you."

The anger faded from her face, and she looked genuinely sympathetic as she stared at him. "Wade, you need to understand that if you keep questioning people who had issues with your sister, you'll never see her the same again. You can't undo that. Think about that before you keep pushing this." With that, she stepped around him and climbed into her vehicle.

Wade stood, processing her warning as she backed out of her parking spot. She was leaving the lot before he crossed the slushy asphalt back to Tika's car.

"Well?" she asked as soon as he was inside.

"She said we should look into Dylan Tyler." He watched her face, gauging her response. Just like the day in HEARTS when he told her who he was, her face sagged, and her eyes widened a little with obvious surprise. "So you know him, then."

"Yeah, I know him."

"Care to expand on that?"

She started the engine. "Not on an empty stomach."

[4]

TIKA TUGGED a wilted lettuce leaf from her cheeseburger and dropped it onto the foil wrapper. The frown on her face wasn't about the limp produce, though. "Dylan Tyler," she said with disgust. "Never thought I'd have to hear that name again."

"What'd he do?" Wade asked as he dug into Lisa's refrigerator.

"It's not what he did, it's what he didn't do." She wiped her fingers clean on a napkin as he took a seat next to her on the couch. The uneasy feeling in her stomach was making her lunch unappealing. She didn't like thinking back on her college years, especially the last one, but those years seemed determined that she was going to face them. She was going to finally slay the demons that she'd been ignoring for far too long.

Wade set two cans of soda and a bottle of hot sauce on the coffee table. Lisa's small dining table was stacked with folded-up boxes, bubble wrap, and other packing materials. Eating at the coffee table was easier.

"Okay," Wade said. "What *didn't* he do?"

She flicked her eyes toward his. A strange emotion toyed across his face. He seemed to be angry, protective, and sympathetic all at the same time. She'd seen that in his eyes before, usually during a conversation about his sister. Though Wade had been the younger sibling, he clearly had been protective of Lisa. Tika couldn't imagine how much it hurt him to hear that there were things that Lisa had done that some would feel were...unethical at best.

Seeing that same underlying sense of protectiveness in his eyes directed toward her did something funny to Tika's stomach. One of the things being part of HEARTS had taught her was that she was responsible for protecting herself, for standing up for herself. But seeing that hard stare in Wade's eyes and the set of his jaw, as if he were ready to bloody his knuckles to protect her, sent a warm sensation through her that settled low in her stomach. She liked the idea of him wanting to defend her.

However, the way her heart skipped was a big warning sign—flickering neon lights reminding her that batting her eyelashes and smiling slyly was an inappropriate response to her client's kindness. Wade was kind and sensitive. Handsome, without a doubt. But he was also paying her to find out what happened the night his sister died. Flirting with the man was about as inappropriate as one could get. And this was her first case. Ever! Talk about unprofessional.

Jerking her attention back to her lunch, Tika stared intently at the condiments oozing out of the side of her sandwich. Clearing her throat, she returned her attention to the topic of their conversation. Dylan Tyler.

"Faculty members weren't the only ones who treated people of color differently at that university," she said. "There were plenty of students who thought most of us only got into the school because the system required minorities to be admitted as well. They felt like they got there on merit while we got there because of Title IX. There was this one guy who always seemed to go out of his way to have problems with a Black or Hispanic classmate. I told Lisa about him and how I was sick of how he treated people —like we were beneath him because he was a rich, white male instead of a commoner. No offense to the white male in the room," she added as she felt warmth touch her cheeks.

"None taken. Not all white males act like that. I certainly don't. But I do know exactly the type of creep you're talking about."

"Anyway, Lisa asked if there had ever been witnesses to his behavior, so I told her about this party I'd gone to. Dylan Tyler stood right next to me and watched this guy harass me for no reason. Dylan stood there with this bewildered look on his face while some jackass told me how I had no right to be at *his* school and attending *his* party."

"Was it his party?"

"No. He was a guest like everyone else. He just felt entitled." She watched Wade lift the top bun off his sandwich and splash the grilled chicken breast in hot sauce until red liquid was spilling over the sides. "What the hell are you doing?"

"Making this taste good." He put his sandwich back together and took a big bite.

She waited for his reaction, which she suspected would be rife with regret. But he closed his eyes and made an exaggerated show of appreciation.

"*Mmmm*," he moaned, causing her to laugh. She didn't mind spicy food, but she couldn't imagine what all that hot sauce would do to her intestines if she'd eaten it. Apparently, he had one of those iron stomachs that could digest anything.

Wade licked sauce from his hand before looking at her again. "I'm sorry for what you went through. We should be more evolved as a society, but sadly we're not. People like that have to push others down to make themselves feel better."

"Or they grew up being told they're superior. Hatred isn't always because people are broken inside, Wade. Some people really do believe they are better because of their skin color." She swallowed down the lecture she was tempted to give. He was doing his best to be supportive of the pain she'd gone through. Lashing out at him wouldn't resolve anything. "When Lisa wrote her story, she listed Dylan Tyler as one of the students responsible for spreading racism on campus because, as she said in her article, being a bystander made him just as guilty."

"Silence is just as damaging in many ways," he agreed.

Tika nodded. "As hard as things were for me, the other people identified in the story got their own brand of harassment. Dylan and the others became targets too. His car was vandalized, he was mocked as he walked through campus, and he withdrew from activities. Eventually, he stopped going to classes. He dropped out weeks before I did."

"You sound like you feel bad about that," Wade said hesitantly.

"No, they got a taste of what they'd been dishing out. But I did feel bad for Dylan. He might have been a complacent coward, but he wasn't a racist. At least not that I ever saw. He was scared. Like the rest of us, I guess."

"Well, he must have gotten over his cowardice. Erin said he'd been threatening Lisa."

Tika creased her brow as she reached for the pile of fries they'd agreed to share instead of ordering two big combination meals neither would finish. "Why would he be threatening her now? All that mess went down years ago."

"I guess the accusations are still following him around. Digging up dirt on people on the Internet isn't hard."

"No, it's not. Any basic background check could tie that article to him. I imagine it is still following him. Did she say how he threatened her?"

Wade wiped a blob of red sauce from the corner of his mouth with the tip of his finger and then licked it clean. "No, but she suggested starting with Lisa's email."

Tika finished chewing the bite in her mouth before saying, "I haven't seen anything from Dylan there, but I'll look again. She has a lot of archived email exchanges and folders within folders. I'm sure her organization was logical to her, but I feel like I'm going in circles trying to make sense of where she placed things. I'm beginning to wonder if that was intentional in case she was ever hacked."

He smiled slightly. "She was always protective of her work until it was ready to be released. And I say protective, but sometimes she bordered on paranoid. She was always worried someone else would break the story before she did. Sometimes she acted like there were people who made it a mission to get in her way."

Tika stared at the fries before selecting one. "Did she ever say that, or did you just get a sense that she was worried about not breaking a story?"

"Just a sense. She was always in a hurry to get the research and put the puzzle together so she could share it with the world."

Tika could see that about Lisa. She had been the same in school. Pushing, pushing, pushing to get to the heart of the matter so she could finally write the story. That must have been something she never outgrew. "I'm going to ask Sam the best way to find out if Lisa had a cloud drive," she said, changing the subject. "I can't find one, but I agree with you. She had to have had a backup somewhere. Did Erin mention anyone else?"

He scowled as he set his sandwich down, but he didn't answer.

"Wade?" she pressed.

He focused much more than necessary as he wiped his hands clean.

She rolled her eyes. "Are you seriously going to make me drag this out of you?"

"She ended things after Lisa used a confidential conversation between them to get leads on a story. Erin's boss traced the story back to her and fired her. She blames Lisa."

Tika pressed her lips together so she didn't point out that Erin was right to. Confidential conversations between someone and their significant other should be sacred, not used for personal gain.

"I'll see if I can find out where Erin was the night Lisa fell," she said.

Wade only considered her question for a moment before shaking his head. "No, I don't think that's necessary."

"We should look into every possibility, Wade."

"Erin is a good person."

Again, Tika stopped herself from blurting out the first thing that came to her mind. "Wade," she said with a more measured voice than the one screaming in her head, "she was angry enough to break up with Lisa. People sometimes act without thinking when they are mad."

"I know that," he said, his voice also calm. Measured.

"So, I should verify—"

"Erin didn't hurt her."

"How can you be so sure?"

He stared at her, his eyes hard as if he couldn't believe she was questioning him.

"You think someone hurt your sister."

"I think someone she was researching for a story hurt her."

Tika nodded. "But you don't think someone who felt betrayed by a story she already wrote could have hurt her?"

"What the hell are you getting at?"

She reminded herself to stay calm. To be the voice of logic here. "You are looking for someone to blame for your sister's untimely death. I understand that. But if you are serious about finding out what happened to Lisa, you can't have a checklist of who you want the villain to be and discount anyone who doesn't fit that criteria."

He pushed himself up and walked away, but Tika didn't let that dissuade her from making her point.

"Erin felt betrayed," she said. "She had a motive. She and Lisa had been dating for a while. Even if she didn't have access to the building, she had to have seen some of the neighbors enough for them to recognize her and let her in. That means she could have been let into the building. You might not like it, but those two things combined warrant me looking into her whereabouts that night."

"I do not want you looking into Lisa's ex."

Standing, she stared wide-eyed. "Well, what do you want?"

"I want the truth!"

"Do you really?" Tika pressed. "Are you sure about that?" She didn't mean to snap, but damn it, he was infuriating her.

"Of course I am!"

"Okay. The truth, Wade, is that your sister was not the upstanding journalist that you always imagined her to be. That's the truth. And if someone was threatening her, it probably wasn't because they were trying to stop her from printing something but because she kicked them in the teeth to get a story. And like it or not, Erin is on that list."

"That's my sister—"

She crossed to him and put her hands on his arms, hoping to make him listen. "Your sister had extremely clouded judgment when it came to protecting her sources."

"This isn't about that article she wrote in college."

"No," she agreed. "It isn't. Because it seems that maybe Lisa didn't learn her lesson in college after all."

Rage lit in his eyes, but Tika didn't back down. He needed to hear this. He needed to understand that he wasn't seeing clearly.

"You have to stop looking at this through the eyes of your grief, Wade," she said more gently. "I know who she was to you, but take a step back and see who she was to other people. Look at how she treated other people. Like they were merely rungs on the ladder of her career. She had to have known she could cause trouble for Erin at work, but she apparently went ahead anyway. Just like she knew she was causing problems for me by sharing my name. And for Dylan Tyler by lumping him in with racists because he was too scared to stand up to a bully."

Wade bit his lips as he put his hands on his hips, effectively removing her hands from his arms. The atmosphere around them grew tense. The sparks that she'd felt earlier were of a different variety now. Nothing about what was bouncing between them was confusing.

His anger was palpable.

"You should go," he said quietly.

She closed her eyes and let out her breath. She hadn't meant to push him so hard. "I'm sorry. I—"

"Tika. Go. Please."

Regret rolled through her. "Wade—"

"Now."

She nodded and whispered, "Okay. I'll call you later."

He gave his head a hard shake. "No. I think... I think I can take it from here. Just send me an invoice for whatever I owe you."

Her heart dropped to her feet. He was firing her? Because she disagreed with him? Because she was trying to make him see he wasn't being reasonable? She must have looked like a fish with her mouth opening and closing as she tried to find the words to convince him to change his mind. Nothing would come out.

After several long seconds, she grabbed her purse from the couch. "I'm sorry," she whispered and headed for the door. Part of her expected him to stop her, to realize he needed her help. But after she opened the door, she turned back. He hadn't even watched her leave. He was still standing with his hands on his hips, but now he had his face down as he seemed to be actively trying to calm himself.

Oh shit. What had she done?

Not only had she just pissed him off, she'd lost a case. Holy shit. Holly was going to kill her. By the time she got to her car, Tika was blinking back tears, and her hands were trembling. As soon as she started her car, she pressed the button to connect her phone to the speaker.

"Call Alexa," she said, then forced herself to swallow at the sound of her voice quivering.

Within moments, her coworker's light-and-happy voice filled her ears. "What's up, chick?"

"I messed up," Tika said, and the tears she'd been trying to fight fell. She wiped her face and exhaled. "Oh my God, Lex, I messed up so bad."

"What happened?" Alexa demanded. Concern replaced the perkiness in her voice, which only made Tika feel worse.

Tika sniffed and swallowed hard before summarizing the blow up. "I told Wade that his sister was a terrible person, and he fired me."

"Oh, baby. Where are you?"

"Sitting outside his sister's apartment building. Crying in my car and looking like a fool." Tika wiped her cheeks again. "Are you working today?"

"I'm working from home. Dean went to visit his sister for the weekend."

Tika huffed out a breath. Dean's sister was in rehab, trying to get clean and get her life together after some pretty traumatic events led her into the depths of addiction. A good reminder that a lot of people had bigger problems than what Tika had just put herself through.

"How's Mandy doing?"

"She's fine. I'm more worried about you right now."

"I have to tell Holly that I got myself fired from my first case. She's going to kill me, Lex."

"No, she's not," Alexa stated. "Holly questioned if she should have intervened from the start. Rene and I convinced her to let you give this a go. This was a mistake we made as a team, Tik. You did your best."

"Should I go to Holly's and tell her face-to-face?"

"She's not home. Sam dragged her and Rene to look at some ballroom somewhere."

Dropping her head back, Tika couldn't help but smile even though she was miserable. Holly's upcoming wedding had been the center of much strife for the HEARTS lately. Holly wanted a simple no-frills wedding. Sam, however, had somehow convinced Holly to let her plan the event and was projecting her own dream wedding onto their boss. Everyone but Sam seemed to see how horribly this was going to turn out.

Holly was being incredibly tolerant right now—not something that any of them were used to—but that wouldn't last forever.

Tika wiped the last of the tears from her eyelashes. "When is Sam going to realize Holly is never going to agree to this fairy-tale wedding?"

"The day that Holly walks in and announces she and Jack got married at city hall like she's wanted to do all along."

"And breaks Sam's wedding-planning heart." The idea of Sam being crushed made Tika hurt for her friend, but Sam was the type who had to get hit over the head with a two-by-four before she listened to something she didn't want to hear. Everyone at HEARTS had heard Holly say over and over that she wanted a small, quiet, and simple wedding. Everyone except Sam.

"Go home, Tik," Alexa said sweetly. "I'll meet you there. Do you want ice cream or liquor?"

Sniffing, Tika weighed the options. "Both."

The local newscaster, a deeply tanned brunette who seemed far too happy to share so much doom and despair, rambled about some civic event that Wade didn't care about. He only had the television on to try to distract himself from replaying his fight with Tika. He didn't care what was happening in the world. Not right now.

He felt like an ass for kicking Tika out the way he had. They were both right, to some extent. He was trying to fit the bad guy into a box, and that was unrealistic. But Tika was wrong to try to force her view of Lisa onto him. She had to respect his relationship with his sister and get over her anger about something Lisa did years ago.

Everyone made mistakes. Everyone was entitled to their own views. But Tika went too far. Erin's statement about Lisa using her was blown out of proportion because of her personal heartache. Wade had no way of knowing the details or what Lisa had really done, but he didn't believe for a second she would have done something that could have hurt Erin. They had been a great couple. Lisa had loved Erin.

Finding out the truth about the threats against Lisa was supposed to be the focus of this investigation, not questioning what kind of person Lisa had been. There was more to her death than a simple stumble down the stairs, but this entire thing was turning into something he hadn't expected.

Clearly Lisa had made mistakes with Tika's story, and maybe she'd made a bad judgment call with whatever Erin had confided to her, but her job was to expose wrongdoing, and Wade refused to believe she did that simply to get ahead.

His attention was drawn to the television when the newscaster said something about Lawrence Butler. Earlier in the morning, Tika had asked Wade if he'd read the article Lisa had written on Lawrence Butler. He'd been so enthralled by the way her light-blue hat contrasted her skin that he'd very nearly blurted out how beautiful he thought she was.

What an idiotic thing to be thinking about the woman he'd hired to help him figure out what had happened to his sister. Things were awkward enough between them given Tika and Lisa's past. Tossing out comments about her looks would definitely not have helped the situation.

Grabbing the remote, he rewound the broadcast a few seconds to get back to the start of the story.

"Congressional candidate Lawrence Butler is facing questions about recent donations to his campaign," the peppy brunette said. "A local political watchdog organization has indicated there are discrepancies in the campaign's reports and documents filed by the candidate. The organization says it was tipped off to the improper financial reports by an unnamed source."

Wade watched a short snippet of a middle-aged politician, probably in his mid-forties, with light hair and a bright smile assuring the flock of reporters that he intended to work with his campaign to determine where the error had occurred. Once they determined the issue, he would do everything in his power to correct any wrongdoing as quickly as possible.

Wade stood taller as puzzle pieces started fitting together in his mind. Lisa had intended to dig deeper into the Butlers. She suspected something about them was off. Earlier, Tika mentioned Lisa had emailed several people, asking about the Butlers, and that those emails had been sent *after* the original article was published.

Lisa had seen through their facade and had started peeling back their masks to see what was hidden underneath. Karen Butler seemed to have caught on and was warning Lisa to back off.

"Common clothes moths pretending to be monarch

butterflies," Wade muttered to himself, repeating what Lisa had said about Butler and his wife.

Wade turned his attention to the black laptop bag next to the sofa as the broadcaster moved onto the next snippet of news. An unnamed source? What if the watchdog organization had been tipped off because Lisa was asking questions about Butler's campaign finances?

Tika indicated that Lawrence Butler was on the list of people she was planning to look into, but to Wade's knowledge, she hadn't gotten very far into her research on the politician. She had gotten distracted by Erin's email.

Damn it. He should have requested Tika to send him a write-up of what she'd done to date. Other than picking on his music and dancing. He laughed softly at the recent memory.

As much as he didn't want to admit it, since he was furious with her, he'd needed those lighthearted moments to get through packing up Lisa's belongings. If Tika hadn't coached him when she'd visited Lisa's apartment, he never would have gotten started. And if she hadn't teased him to lift his spirits, he likely wouldn't have been able to finish packing up Lisa's clothing.

There was no way for him to know if Tika had sensed how much he needed the distraction or if simply having her near him was enough. He suspected it might have been a little of both. Either way, part of him already regretted that he'd turned away the peace she brought to him. That sense of inner calm was not something he came by easily in the last few weeks.

The temptation to call her and apologize was strong, however, he suspected if he reached out to her right now, he'd mention the news story about the Butler campaign. The last thing he wanted was for her to think he was trying to make amends simply to get her to research the case. He was sorry they had butted heads and that he'd fired her without considering her side of things. Their attempt to talk things out shouldn't be clouded by this particular turn of events.

"Worry about that later," he muttered to himself as he stretched to grab the laptop. Pulling Lisa's portable computer from the padded bag, he flipped the top up and waited for the device to boot up.

The sticky note with the passwords HEARTS had set up was stuck to the top of Lisa's laptop, but he didn't need to read it since they had chosen the most simplistic number combination possible as the new login. As soon as the screen appeared prompting him to enter the username and password, he did so by memory and nervously tapped his fingers as he waited for access.

Once the laptop was ready, waiting for Wade's next command, he froze.

Erin had warned him that digging into Lisa's work was going to change his view of her. Tika warned him that he should let this go before he learned something about Lisa he couldn't forget. What if they were right? What if Lisa's ambition made her do things that were in the gray area of journalistic ethics?

He didn't want to consider the possibility that they could be right, but part of him couldn't deny it.

He shook his head hard to rid his mind of those thoughts. He knew his sister better than anyone. She wasn't perfect by any means, but she did her best. Her career had been about helping people. She had been an amazing person. He didn't doubt that.

So why was he hesitating now? Why was he second guessing?

With renewed determination, he logged into Lisa's email and did a search for *Butler* in her inbox. Several emails filled the screen. Including one from Karen Butler.

Opening the correspondence, Wade read the text several times, seeing between the lines more and more with every pass. On the surface, Karen Butler seemed to be gently telling Lisa there would be no further interviews offered to her. According to Karen, Lawrence Butler's campaign manager felt it was important that he focus on more "mainstream" journalists. Karen very much appreciated Lisa's recent efforts to discuss "certain events," but she and her husband were focusing on the future, not the past.

However, should Lisa want to discuss Butler's stance on key issues, they would be able to find time for that.

Though she didn't come right out and say it, Karen was clearly saying Lisa wouldn't be given press passes to any further events unless she stopped asking about something in the Butler's past.

"Certain events," Wade muttered as he dissected the clear threat. However, this wasn't the kind of threat he had been looking to find. This was the kind that was warning Lisa she would be shut out from covering Butler's political career in the future.

Okay. So Lisa had uncovered something about Lawrence's past his wife didn't like. But what? What had she discovered? What was she looking into? How did that tip off some political watchdog group about issues with Butler's finances?

What the hell was he supposed to do now?

Call Tika. He had to call Tika. Because he was in over his head and had no idea what step he should take next.

He stared at his cell phone for at least three minutes, debating what he would say when—*if*—she answered. Finally, he blew out a heavy breath and snatched up his phone. The moment he selected her contact information and connected the call, he started pacing.

The ringing stopped, and his end of the call filled with the sound of shushing.

"Shhh, I need to answer this," Tika said.

Wade tilted his head, trying to make out what the woman in the background was saying, but half of her words seemed to be in Spanish. And slightly slurred.

Tika cleared her throat and said in a voice so calm it was obviously forced. "Hello?"

"Hey, Tika. It's Wade."

"I know. Your number is in my contacts."

He considered her response. She'd shared the odd kind of honesty that comes with too much alcohol. Combined with the slurring voice in the background and Tika's measured greeting convinced Wade that he had interrupted her girls' night. He didn't know her well, but he could picture her sitting around with a group of friends, drinking and complaining about how hardheaded he could be. For some reason, that made his frustration with her lessen even more.

"Tika?" he asked as a grin tugged at his lips.

"Yes?"

"Are you drunk?"

"*No.* Why would you ask that?"

His smile widened. "Because you are obviously drunk right now."

Her side of the phone would be quiet if not for the other person asking what he was saying. "I had some wine," she answered after a few seconds. "But I'm not drunk."

"Yes, you are," her companion sang, only to be hushed again.

Wade's uneasiness eased. "It's not even dinnertime yet."

Tika was quiet for a moment before enunciating each word. "I have had a long day, and I deserve to have a glass of wine if I want one."

"One?" he teased.

"Several."

He laughed. "You are right. You deserve a drink. I was an ass earlier, and I wanted to tell you that I'm sorry I snapped at you."

"I'm sorry too," she rushed to reply. "I was a jerk. I shouldn't have said what I said."

"Lisa clearly made mistakes," he admitted, "but you have to understand that she's my sister and—"

"I have no right to say bad things about her to your face."

Reclaiming his seat on the couch, he said, "I'd prefer if you didn't say them behind my back, either, but I suppose that's too much to ask."

"Can, um, can we talk about that tomorrow, because I can probably come up with a better response then?"

"Yeah," he said softly. "We'll talk tomorrow. Tika?"

"Huh?"

"Do yourself a favor and drink some water. Hangovers are no fun."

"I will. Thanks for calling, Wade."

He ended the call and sank back on the couch. The tension that had been sitting low in his gut all afternoon finally eased, and he could breathe again. They'd talk again tomorrow. Tomorrow they could settle the disagreement between them. They could start fresh. And hopefully, she could help him make sense of this latest bit of information—if there was any sense to be made.

[5]

Tᴉᴋᴀ ǫᴜɪᴇᴛʟʏ ᴛᴀʟᴋᴇᴅ to herself as she walked toward the secured entrance to Lisa's apartment building. "Hey, Wade, it's me," she said brightly, and then tried again, enunciating the words with a softer please-forgive-me tone. Neither greeting sounded as calm and casual as it should have.

She shook her head and immediately regretted it. Damn Alexa and her excellent taste in wine. The drinks had gone down much too easily as Tika had sat on her sofa crying and trying to justify why Wade shouldn't have fired her. She couldn't really remember the reasons she'd given her coworker, but Tika was certain they had to have been good. And valid. Though she did wish she had written them down because all she could seem to think of this morning was how much her head hurt.

After he had called her the previous evening, she'd turned the topic to how she was going to take a new approach to this case to ensure he wouldn't regret reaching out to her. Again, she wished she had written her ideas down, because she couldn't really remember what she'd come up with.

Even though Wade had reminded her to drink water so she didn't dehydrate from the alcohol, she hadn't listened. In the excitement of getting a second chance, she had continued to drink just as much wine, just as fast as she had when she'd been miserable over being fired. She knew better than to drink so much, but she still hadn't taken his advice. No doubt he'd take a little bit of pleasure in her pain. He had certainly sounded amused by her state of mind when he'd called her.

As she neared the main door to the building, someone walked out. Tika wasn't surprised when the man held the door instead of letting it close and lock behind him as he should have since he didn't know Tika. As a matter of fact, she couldn't recall seeing him once since she'd been frequenting the building with Wade. He had mentioned that one of Lisa's concerns was the lack of security. That had added to his certainty that anyone could have gotten into her building the night she had fallen.

Tika couldn't disagree with Lisa's concerns. She had already realized that most of the residents tended to choose friendliness over safety. Though she didn't recognize the man, he smiled and nodded as she walked by him as if she belonged in the building.

"Thank you," she said on her way inside. The door closed behind her, and the audible click of the lock sounded. What a false sense of security that must have provided to the many single and elderly residents. They must have thought, on some level, that the locked door could keep trouble out, though, like Lisa, they must have been aware the measure of safety was useless when the neighbors didn't utilize it properly.

As Tika walked to the elevator, she considered how easy it would have been for someone to slip unnoticed into the building the night Lisa died. All it would have taken would have been the patience to stand by and wait for someone else to enter or exit.

Trying to determine if there was a way to find out if someone held the door kept her mind occupied during the short ride to the fourth floor. Tika stepped out of the elevator before she thought to let Wade know she had arrived. However, as she neared Lisa's apartment, the door opened, and Wade stepped out carrying a black trash bag.

He stopped in his tracks when he saw her. A hint of a smile played across his mouth, and she wasn't sure if he was happy to see her or if his amusement from the night before had been reignited.

"Hey."

"Hey," she said. "I'm sorry to just drop by, but—"

"No," he rushed to say. Moving aside, he gestured for her to enter Lisa's apartment. "Let me toss this down the garbage chute, and I'll be right back."

She walked into the apartment and marveled at how much had changed in the last few days. The first time she'd been here, Wade hadn't even begun to pack. Now the apartment was almost empty. Boxes were stacked against one wall. The bookshelves were bare, and the wall hangings had been removed.

If Tika didn't know better, she'd think Wade was excitedly moving on to a new place, a new adventure. Sadly, he had found a storage unit to keep his deceased sister's belongings where they would sit untouched until sometime in the future when he was ready to part with them.

He had made a lot of progress since she'd left him there yesterday. Perhaps his frustration after their disagreement had been a big motivator. While she'd been drinking and crying on Alexa's shoulder, he'd been moving even closer to letting go of the life he'd shared with his sister. Guilt touched Tika's soul again. She should have been here for him. She should have been here to tease him and ease the pain he certainly had felt as he put Lisa's belongings into boxes.

The apartment had a completely different feeling with all the wall hangings missing and the knickknacks packed away.

She turned when the door opened and he came inside the apartment empty handed. The uncertainty on his face made her want to hug him. He was definitely feeling as uneasy about their argument as she was.

"All packed, huh?" she asked gently.

He nodded as sadness touched his eyes. "Movers will be here tomorrow, and then...that's it."

"I'm sorry," she whispered. "I can't imagine how hard this is for you. I know I didn't make things any easier for you yesterday."

"Hey," he said before she could delve into her well-practiced apology. "Tensions are high right now. I'm a little more sensitive than I normally would be with"—he gestured around the empty apartment—"all this. I shouldn't have snapped."

"You just lost your sister, Wade. You have every right to

be sensitive, especially when I was completely out of line by taking Erin's side."

"It's behind us," he said. "I'm glad you're here. How are you feeling?"

She made a show of scrunching up her face. "Not too bad. Thanks for the reminder to rehydrate."

He tilted his head and smirked as he searched her eyes—or, more likely, took an assessment of her blotchy skin and bloodshot eyes. "Did you listen?"

"No," she admitted with a forced smile, hoping to hide some of her misery. Her head ached. Her stomach wouldn't stop rolling.

He laughed but was kind enough to do so quietly. "I can tell. You're moving a little slower today. I'd offer you coffee, but..."

"Packed?" she figured based on the fact that the kitchen counter was empty, save for a box with Wade's handwriting identifying the contents of the box.

He nodded once in confirmation. "Packed."

She shrugged. "I'll recover."

"I can offer you water." He snapped his lips closed and lifted his finger the moment he finished speaking as he obviously came to a realization. "But not a glass. You'd have to drink from the tap. Perhaps you'd like a can of soda?"

"No thanks. I'm good. I only came by to apologize to you face-to-face."

Wade shook his head, and his posture softened. Once again, the man looked like he was on the verge of defeat. She hated seeing him like that. When he was able to put the circumstances surrounding his sister out of his mind for a minute or two, there was a mischievous light in his eyes that Tika thought must have made him a favorite among his students. He was probably one of those science teachers who, rather than answering questions, suggested the class put on their goggles for an experiment or led his students outside with a list of things to find to help them better understand photosynthesis or some other nerdy thing.

"It's done," Wade said in a soft voice. "Let's move on, okay?"

Though she worried that it wasn't done, it wasn't over, and it would come back around, she wasn't in the mood to push. She didn't have the mental energy or clarity to work through some underlying resentments. "Okay. So...I'm unfired?"

He pursed his lips together and furrowed his brow as if he were considering his options. Finally, he relaxed his face into a soft smile and nodded. "Yeah, I guess. You are officially unfired."

The final bit of anxiety that had been squeezing her chest eased, and she took a deep breath. "Good."

"And since you are back on the case," Wade said as he sat on the couch, "did you happen to watch the news last night?"

Tika set her bag on the coffee table as she eased down next to him with a hint of a grin on her lips. "Uh, no. I was otherwise occupied."

"Right," he muttered with his own grin. However, his grin faded as he met her gaze. "There was a story about Lawrence Butler."

Her amusement also ended as she sat taller and tilted her

head. He had definitely piqued her curiosity. That name just kept popping up. "What about him?"

"Some watchdog group is looking into his campaign finances. They were tipped off about something. From someone."

"Lisa?" she asked.

He shrugged. "It could have been, but I guess there's really no way of knowing without talking to them. I searched through Lisa's emails. She was definitely looking into something. Karen Butler sent an email with a thinly veiled 'you'll never interview me or my husband again' statement. She or someone else on Butler's team was not happy with Lisa."

Tika nodded. "Okay. I'll move them to the top of my list to look into. I haven't found anything on her phone or social media. We have got to find her cloud drive."

"Have you looked through her browser history?"

"Yes, and I can't find anything. I need to dig deeper. I know it seems like we've been searching forever, but really it's only been a few days, and there are lots of emails, messages, and browsing history to get through. We've only scratched the surface of her inbox, Wade. I'm working backward because—"

"I trust you," he said before she could list off the reasons for her approach.

The simple statement allowed her to relax. Keeping her investigation transparent and being more considerate of his feelings were the best things she could do right now. The last thing she wanted was to have another disagreement with him. Or get fired again. Next time, she might not be so lucky. He might not be willing to forgive her without more groveling.

"I'm glad," she said. "I really am."

Wade put his hand on hers, and Tika felt the contact heat her entire body. That reaction was dangerous. Like playing with matches in a fireworks store. But she didn't pull back. Instead, she held her breath and turned her palm up to meet his. They entwined their fingers, and her chest grew tight, but not with anxiety this time. This was something completely different, and she refused to try to name it.

"I know this has been awkward for you," Wade said with a gentle tone, as if to reassure her. "I sincerely appreciate that you've tried to put that aside to help me. You didn't have to. I know that. You're a good person, Tika."

"So are you, Wade. You're a really good person. Lisa was so lucky to have a brother like you." She stopped herself before adding that she wished Lisa had been more like him. She wished Lisa had been more considerate and patient. Maybe she wouldn't have made so many enemies if she hadn't always been doing that pushing thing that must have come so naturally to her.

He looked away, and she sensed he understood she'd wanted to say something else but had chosen not to. He probably even understood what it was she hadn't said.

Quiet settled between them. That sensation of the danger of playing with matches and fireworks grew to the point she could no longer ignore it. As wrong as it felt, there was an underlying attraction between them. She was certain he felt the same, but the fear that he didn't made her keep her observation to herself. If he didn't feel the same, at best she'd be making an ass out of herself. At worst, she'd get herself fired twice in as many days.

Finally, because she didn't know what else to do, Tika slid her hand from his. "I should go and let you finish—"

"Wait," he stated, almost sounding terrified that she planned to leave. "Do you think you can do something for me?"

Her nerves lit. The atmosphere around them was different now, somehow more aware but less connected. She wasn't sure what he could need, but anxiety poked at her heart. Maybe he had sensed their attraction as well and was about to tell her to send one of her coworkers next time. Maybe he didn't want her working with him after all.

"Of course. Whatever you need."

Wade looked around the room. "After the movers come tomorrow, I have to hand the keys over to the building manager and won't have any reason to be here ever again. I don't have to tell you what a struggle that's going to be. I spent a lot of time here with my sister. We made really great memories here, and I feel like I'm leaving a big part of her behind. After tomorrow..."

A mix of relief and sadness settled over her. Tika was certain she knew where he was headed, and it wasn't asking her to disappear and never return. This had nothing to do with her. Or the feelings they seemed to be trying to ignore.

She didn't push. She let him work through his request on his own.

"I need to..." He scoffed, as if frustrated with himself, and his cheeks blushed. He swallowed hard, took a deep breath, and straightened his shoulders before looking into her eyes. "I need to see where she fell. I need to face that part of losing her, but I can't seem to make myself go into that stairwell. I keep thinking about how you made boxing up her things easiest, and I thought... Do you think you could..."

"Yes," she whispered. "Yes, I'll help you."

He nodded but the agony didn't seem to ease. "Now?"

Her heart ached at the idea of how much this would hurt him, but she understood his need. When her grandfather had passed away unexpectedly in his sleep, Tika had felt an unnatural pull deep inside her until she finally gave in and went to his home. She had stood at the foot of his bed, knowing he'd died there, thinking of how much she would miss him. That was the first real step she'd taken in accepting his loss, so she understood Wade's need.

Tika reclaimed his hand as she stood and waited for him to stand beside her before guiding him to the door. Wade tightened his grip on her hand as they walked down the hallway, but his hold became almost painful as they stopped in front of the stairwell door. Her heart started racing so hard, the beating was almost painful. Anxiety danced along her nerves like a fast-spreading wildfire. Breathing became difficult.

As difficult as this was for her to be standing beside him during this process, she knew the sensations had to be magnified for him. She watched his face, doing her best to read his mind so she could give him whatever he needed to get through the next few minutes.

Wade reached for the knob, gripped it, but he didn't open the door. After several moments, Tika gently removed his hand, turned the knob, and pulled the door open just a few inches. Just enough to start the process.

The despair on his face as he slowly opened the door was

enough to make her wish she had waited and let him do this in his own time, but then he took one step, and another, until they were standing at the top of the stairs where Lisa had fallen.

A tear slid down Wade's cheek as he stared at the landing below them, undoubtedly imagining the scene that had unfolded there. How Lisa must have tumbled, how she had probably screamed. How she must have landed helplessly at the bottom of these stairs.

Tika bit her lips as tears threatened to spill from her as well. She wanted to focus on helping him, being strong for him, and would allow her emotions to hit her later.

Wade squeezed her hand even tighter. "When we were kids, this older boy used to steal my toys right out of my hands. One day, I was on my bike, and he made me wreck. Then he laughed as he went for a ride. When I got home with scrapes on my knees and elbows, Lisa demanded to know what had happened, so I told her.

"She took me back outside and then hid behind a tree and waited for him. As soon as he showed up and tried to take my toys, she jumped out screaming like a lunatic, telling him how she would make his life a living hell if he ever even looked at me again." He smiled at the memory. "He tried to act like he wasn't scared, but he never stole my stuff again. She was always a protector. *Always.*"

His lips quivered, and he blinked rapidly as he tore his gaze from the stairs and faced Tika. "Someone hurt her," he whispered. "Someone took her from me. I know that. I can feel it." He put his hand to his heart. "I can *feel* it."

"We're going to find out what happened to her," Tika answered.

A sob left him and echoed around them. She hushed him as another tear fell down his cheek. He pulled her against him and buried his face in her shoulder as he hugged her close. She returned his hold, doing her best to comfort him. She had no way of knowing how long he clung to her, but she didn't dare pull away until he did.

He sniffed and wiped his face. "I'm sorry."

"Don't be," she insisted before he could go on. "I'm here for you, Wade."

"Not for this."

"For whatever you need," she insisted.

"Thanks," he said quietly. He looked back down at the landing before shaking his head. "She hit the wall so hard, her skull fractured."

"Shh." Tika put her hand on his cheek. "Don't do that to yourself."

"I can see it even if I don't say it. I still know how she died, Tik. I just don't know why."

Her heart ached as his voice cracked. No matter how many times she had said she understood his need to find out if Lisa's death was an accident, she hadn't. Until that moment. Until she saw the raw pain in his eyes as he looked at her. She hadn't gotten it, not really. Because she hadn't wanted to feel that deeply for the loss of someone who had hurt her. How selfish was that?

"I'm going to find out," she whispered. "I swear to you. I will find out."

Wade hugged her closer to him again, and she held on,

this time without the resentments she had allowed to linger in her heart. Lisa Steele was a reporter, she was ambitious. Maybe she was even manipulative, but she was more than that. She was a sister. She was a daughter. She was a person who had been loved and deserved to be honored as such.

And her death, if it was more than an accident, deserved to be investigated.

Stroking her hand over his hair, Tika held him as he grieved for his loss.

"I *am* going to find out," she said with a determination she hadn't had before.

WADE ACCEPTED THE CUP OF HOT TEA TIKA SAT IN front of him. Since he'd packed up all of Lisa's appliances, including the coffeemaker, Tika had insisted they go to the coffee shop around the corner from Lisa's apartment. She wanted a cup of coffee, and he hadn't had the strength to argue. In fact, he was convinced the real reason she wanted to go to the coffee shop was to get him out of Lisa's apartment for a while.

He hadn't really allowed himself to feel the depth of his loss. His parents had been a wreck from the time Lisa had been rushed to the hospital. The medical staff had been kind but honest. A week after her lingering in a coma with no signs of life, they made it clear as gently as possible that they needed to let Lisa go.

Wade had never seen his parents crumble like they had that day. Or the days following. He'd pushed his pain aside, braced himself as much as he could, and stepped up to carry as much of their burdens as he could. Now that he could put that weight down, he was starting to feel all the devastation he had ignored.

He didn't know how he could have possibly moved forward with the things he had if Tika hadn't helped him. There was no possible way for him to tell her how grateful he was for that.

But he guessed a cup of coffee was a good start.

"Thanks," he said when she sat across from him and cradled her paper cup.

"You're welcome." She looked around the little shop for several seconds before meeting his gaze. "I owe you an apology."

He shook his head. "No. We're past that, remember?"

"I don't mean the disagreement yesterday. I mean...I didn't allow myself to see this through your eyes. I don't know if that was because of my past with Lisa or because I didn't want to allow myself to feel the pain that I knew you were feeling. Maybe I just didn't want to get emotionally involved. This is a tough job sometimes," she admitted. "Holly and Rene are really good at distancing themselves from their emotions. Alexa is good at comforting her clients and soothing them. Eva has a good balance of both. I guess I haven't figured out where I fall on that scale, but I'm pretty sure that I held on to my anger at Lisa more than I should have so that I didn't have to feel your loss. And for that, I'm sorry."

Wade took a few seconds to process her admission before nodding. "I can understand your hesitancy to let your emotions be impacted by your cases. I imagine you're tasked with telling a lot of people that their spouse is having an affair.'"

She widened her eyes dramatically before she rolled her head back and mouthing *OMG*. "I have had to witness so much adultery, I swear to God, I have nightmares about people cheating on each other."

He smiled. "Nightmares about adultery? I'm not sure how that could play out."

"Cheap motels, cheaper women, even cheaper liquor."

He held up his hand. "Say no more. Please. I'm there. I get it now, and I have many regrets for asking."

She chuckled as she shook her head. "Not as many as me."

Reaching across the table, he held out his hand. He was almost afraid she wasn't going to take it, but after several heartbeats, she put her palm to his. "Thank you for today, Tika. I can't explain why I needed to see where she got hurt, but I did. I can't imagine having done it without you there to support me."

"Of course."

"This has been unbelievably hard on my parents. I'm doing my best to be strong for them."

Sympathy filled her eyes and made his heart ache, but not necessarily in a bad way. This felt like the kind of ache that went with healing, with having that one person there who understood.

"You're doing amazing, Wade," she said.

"I hope so."

"What, um, what do your parents think about you investigating threats against Lisa?"

"They don't know," he said.

Tika widened her eyes as she sat back. "They don't?"

He shook his head. Guilt wasn't how he'd describe the feeling in his gut, but he had to admit keeping this from his parents didn't feel quite right. "I can't tell them her death might have been foul play until I know for sure. Or at least until I get enough information to get the police involved. Right now, I just... I can't add any more stress for them. Do you know what I mean?" he asked, fearing that his justification wasn't as logical as he had convinced himself.

"I do," she said. "I get it."

He frowned. "I don't think Mom could handle the idea of someone hurting Lisa. I have to know for certain before I break her heart even further."

Tika brushed her thumb over his hand as her eyes reflected the sadness he felt. She was the first person he had felt comfortable sharing all of this with. He had friends and relatives that would be there for him without question, but he had hesitated in talking to them. Tika, however, seemed to make him need to share.

"I think keeping this from them is for the best," she said, her voice filled with kindness.

"Thank you." He focused on her touch, using it to keep him grounded. "I needed that reassurance. I know I've asked a lot from you, but I'm wondering if you might do something else for me."

"What?"

Turning his eyes to hers, he debated if he had the right to ask but realized how much he needed Tika's support. "There's an awards dinner Tuesday night. It's the last award that Lisa is likely to ever be nominated for. My parents were invited to attend, but they aren't ready for that. I told them I would go on their behalf and accept the award if she gets it. Would you go with me? I'm not sure I can do this alone."

"Yes," she said without seeming to consider his request. "Of course."

"This isn't part of the investigation. I'm asking you to attend because I want you there with me." His stomach churned as he realized that he'd basically just asked her on a date.

She smiled sweetly. "I understand that. And I'm still happy to go."

"Good." He smiled too. "I have to wear a suit, so it's kind of dressy. Not super dressy, though," he quickly added.

"Spoken like a high school teacher."

Wade leaned back, but he didn't release her hand. He liked holding her hand. Rolling his eyes for effect, he enunciated out his words to mimic the teenagers he spent his days enlightening. "Yeah, it's like *homecoming* dressy, not *prom* dressy."

Tika laughed, and the stress in his chest eased. He was so glad they had worked things out. Not only because he did trust her to find out what happened to Lisa, but because having her close eased his sorrow. He wanted to be near her. Maybe even take her on a real date. Not to a journalistic awards dinner or a little café where they were sipping hot drinks while he tried to unsee the spot where his sister died.

"Hey," Tika said, tugging at his hand.

He focused on her face. "Sorry, I faded, didn't I?"

"A little bit. Are you okay?"

"Yeah, I mean...why wouldn't I be?"

That understanding smile of hers returned. "Tell me about this award Lisa is up for."

"She wrote an article about a local company that still subscribed to that good ol' boys' mentality. Very few women made executive positions, and those who did quickly moved on to other companies. Sexual harassment was acceptable and, from what Lisa had found, almost expected. They were trapped in the fifties or something," he said with a slight laugh. "Lisa found out and exposed them. They had to go through a complete overhaul. A lot of upper management was let go. All as a result of her article." His pride swelled again. "She was so good at what she did."

He flicked his eyes to Tika. Instead of that look of doubt she tended to have when he commented on Lisa's abilities as a journalist, she nodded.

"I know she was," she said. "She was an amazing journalist, Wade. And you have every reason to be proud of her." She offered him a sympathetic smile as she squeezed his hand. "I know I've been a bit resentful ever since her past actions resurfaced into my life, but you have to understand that she turned my life upside down. It's taken reevaluating everything to realize that I ended up where I belong. I belong at HEARTS, and I wouldn't have found my way there if Lisa hadn't written that article."

Finally, he felt like Tika had let the past go. The relief washed over him like a wave. He hadn't realized how much he needed to hear Tika accept that Lisa was a good person. He smiled and let out a big breath, feeling like a huge amount of stress had eased.

"I'm glad you've found a way to forgive her."

Tika laughed lightly. "Okay, I haven't gotten that far yet. I'm just starting to let go of the anger enough to see that it wasn't done with malice."

Wade started to respond, but Tika tugged his hand.

"Give me a little more time, Wade. I've had a few years of finding all the ways she screwed me over. I'm working through it, okay?"

"Okay," he said. Though he felt a bit of disappointment nagging at him, he did his best to let it go.

[6]

Tika jerked back the dressing room curtain and walked to the platform placed in front of a half circle of mirrors. This was the sixth dress she'd tried on at this shop, but she'd lost count of how many times she had changed at the previous boutiques she'd visited. The knee-length satin was the same robin's-egg blue as her knitted hat, the one Wade had complimented.

He said he liked how the cool hue looked against her skin, and she had nearly melted in her car seat like a schoolgirl when he'd said that. A schoolgirl crush wasn't far from what she'd been feeling for him. The phrase *hot for teacher* popped into her mind, but she shook it loose and focused on the mirror.

She ran her hand over the lace-covered bodice. "Is this too much?"

Sam looked up from Lisa's laptop. Tika had lured Sam to the boutique under the pretenses of shopping...which wasn't a complete falsity. She didn't have a cocktail dress to wear to the awards dinner with Wade, but she also wanted Sam's help in trying to figure out if Lisa had accessed a cloud drive. She still hadn't been able to find one in her browser history. While Tika tried on dress after dress, Sam pecked away on the keyboard, working her cyber voodoo.

She'd also been trying to find any hidden files or tucked-away threats that Tika may have missed. With this being Tika's first actual investigation, she was paranoid she'd miss something crucial. The other HEARTS had said more than once that missing the forest for the trees was far too easy sometimes.

"Absolutely not," Sam stated. "It's perfect. Subtle but sexy."

Tika tugged the cap sleeves into place. "I'm not going for sexy," Tika said, but even she didn't believe the denial. The material was too low-cut in the front to be anything but sexy. She'd have to be certain to find slip-on shoes, because if she had to bend over to buckle straps, the dress didn't stand a chance at keeping her breasts contained. They'd spill over the scalloped neckline without an ounce of resistance. Not to mention bending over would definitely run a risk of the hemline rising far above acceptable heights.

Sam pressed her lips together and smirked. "Yeah. Okay."

Facing her friend and coworker, Tika stared hard. "He's a client."

Sam snorted. "Like that's ever stopped anyone on our team before."

Tika couldn't argue. Alexa and Rene had fallen for clients while working cases. Holly liked to remind everyone how unethical such behavior was but had yet to put any kind of formal rule into place. Besides, she had met her fiancé on a case, too, but he hadn't been a client. He'd been a detective assisting with her case. Just as Joshua had been assisting Eva on her case when they had gotten back together.

Things between Wade and Tika were different, though. They weren't working some high-stress dangerous case together. The biggest challenge for them was that Tika saw Lisa's career in a slightly different light than Wade. He'd never stop admiring his big sister, and Tika would never be able to. Sure, Lisa used her writing for the greater good, but even after the lessons she should have learned when her article on racism went wrong, she seemed to have had no hesitations in stepping on people, and that didn't sit well with Tika.

Likely because she'd been one of the rungs Lisa had used to climb her career ladder. And then she'd been tossed aside and forgotten as if the pain Lisa had caused didn't matter. As if *Tika* hadn't mattered. The hopes and dreams Tika had were just things cast aside so Lisa could reach her goals. No matter how much Tika tried to forgive, she couldn't.

"I can't let it go," she blurted out.

"Can't let what go?"

Sitting next to Sam on the bench, she frowned as she tugged the hem of her dress down. She'd definitely have to be mindful of sitting if she bought this outfit. There was a fine line between looking attractive for her date and screaming out in desperation to be noticed.

Heaving a sigh, Tika shrugged. "This deep-seated anger I have at Lisa is still like a...like a volcano ready to erupt. It's lessened, so I'm not as angry as I was, but I keep finding confirmation that she really was the type of person who would have intentionally given up a source to save her own ass. I don't want to feel that way, but I do. That isn't fair to Wade. He loved her. I have no doubt she was a wonderful sister, but I just can't stop thinking that at her core, she was a terrible person who didn't care who she burned as long as she came out ahead. That's a terrible thing to think about someone who may have been murdered."

"Who may have been murdered because she didn't care who she burned as long as she came out ahead," Sam pointed out. "You weren't the only one that she stabbed in the back, Tika. This seemed to be an ongoing theme with her, and whether she meant to or not, she ruined your chance at having the life you'd always dreamed of. You don't have to get over that just because you like her brother."

"*Hey*. I never said I like Wade."

"Girl, please," Sam muttered. "Get the blue dress. I have a jewelry set that will go perfectly with it. What are you going to do with your hair?"

"He likes it down." As soon as the words were out of her mouth, Tika gasped. Not just because she had said that but because she knew it to be true by the way Wade looked at her when her curly hair was falling around her face. He always stared at her a little longer, and his smile was a little sweeter. "Oh my God. I didn't mean it like that."

Sam threw her head back and laughed. "Tik, admit he's adorable."

She didn't want to. She even took a breath to deny it. But the truth refused to be denied. Grinning, Tika said, "He is. He's incredibly adorable."

"And you like him."

Tika stuck her lip out in a forced pout. "I do. Damn it. I didn't want to. This is my first big case, Sam. I can't fall for my client on my first case."

"Just because you like him doesn't mean you have to set aside your professionalism. You can date him *after* you wrap up his case."

Tika eyed her friend. "Who are you? Since when are you even remotely logical? You should be telling me to nail him, ethics be damned."

Sam shrugged and her face sagged. "I'm trying to be less...*me*. I think I've gotten on Holly's nerves too much lately."

Thoughts of Wade's sexy smile faded as soon as Tika saw the misery on Sam's face. Concern for her friend grew when Sam looked away and exhaled slowly. Sam didn't let things get to her. She was an ace at brushing this off and moving on.

"Why? What happened?"

"Nothing specific. She just seems really short with me these days."

Tika nudged her slightly. "It's Holly. When isn't she short with you? With everyone? It's her nature. You know she adores you."

"Does she?" Sam shook her head. "I don't think so, Tik. I'm not like the rest of you. You guys are smart and serious—"

Tika's stomach twisted. She'd never seen Sam be anything but confident. This self-doubt surprised Tika, and she didn't like it. Sam had a naturally spunky persona. Sunlight seemed to burst from her. Usually in the form of sarcasm, but she still lit up a room without trying. Seeing her down on herself was so out of character that Tika was genuinely concerned.

"You *are* brilliant." Tika gestured toward the laptop. "Would I trust you with this if you weren't? Eva can do basic computer hacking, but you...you are a master who would be absolutely terrifying if you started to use your powers for evil." Tika smiled when Sam snorted and rolled her eyes. Wrapping her arm around Sam's shoulders, she gave her a half-hug. "It'll pass. Whatever it is. Maybe just back off the wedding planning. I know your heart is in the right place, but let her have the casual day she wants. If she regrets it later, that's her burden to carry. Not yours."

Sam frowned. "I just want her to have a really beautiful day. She and Jack deserve that after all they've been through."

"I agree, but if Holly doesn't want that, then you should respect that. Stop pressing her to do something more than she wants."

"Maybe I should."

"Holly's rough around the edges, Sam, but she would die for you. For any of us. You know she would."

Sam nodded. "I know. But being on her bad side is a scary place."

"You're not on her bad side."

"I live on her bad side, Tika." Before Tika could argue, Sam forced a big smile to her face. "Hey, enough of that. Let's talk about this dress. You look hot. We need to get you some killer stilettos. I've yet to meet a man who didn't have a secret shoe fetish."

Tika laughed. "He might have a secret shoe fetish, but I

have to walk in them. Let's be reasonable. I'm going to get changed. You figure that damn cloud drive out."

She left Sam to work her magic as she put her street clothes back on and slid the dress onto a hanger. By the time she returned, Sam was smirking like a freaking Cheshire cat. Tika smiled too because that could only mean one thing. She'd found Lisa's cloud drive.

"Well?"

"First, you owe me lunch. Agree."

"Agreed."

"Second, you're wearing stilettos."

Tika frowned. "Are you seriously blackmailing my footwear?"

"With sparkles on them."

"Fine. Sparkly stilettos and lunch."

Sam turned Lisa's phone screen toward Tika. "See this app icon?"

Tika leaned closer and narrowed her eyes. "Yeah?"

"The reason you couldn't find a cloud drive in her browser history is because she doesn't have an online cloud drive, which if you think about it is very smart." She tapped her temple and winked. "Those servers get hacked all the time. They aren't nearly as safe as they should be."

"I don't care about that," Tika said. "What's this icon?"

"Lisa had a personal cloud drive, Tik." She clicked the app, and it opened to a site that prompted the user to log in. "She goes to this page, connects her laptop or phone or whatever digital device she's using, and tells it to transfer her data to a private server somewhere."

Tika's heart sank. "Somewhere?"

"Don't look so sad, sweet girl," Sam said with a faux maternal tone. "The server would have to have an Internet connection to receive data and a power source. It's probably at her apartment."

Hope lit Tika up for a moment, but then she frowned again. "Wade has already packed up her apartment. The movers are there right now."

"Where are they taking her things?"

"To a storage unit."

"Well, at least you have a starting point now." Sam stood and put Lisa's devices into the bright-red bag she always carried, then put the strap over her shoulder. A sly grin curved her lips. "You are going to be the best distraction a brother in mourning has ever had."

"Or I'm going to make an ass out of myself by dressing far too sexy for an awards dinner for his deceased sister." As soon as she said it, she looked at the dress. "No. I'm not getting this."

"Yes, you are," Sam insisted. "Even sad men appreciate sexy women."

Tika laughed softly. "You are such a troublemaker," she muttered.

"But I'm right," Sam practically sang as she took the dress from Tika.

As they walked to the cashier, Tika texted Wade, asking if he remembered packing a personal server with Lisa's belongings. She was waiting for her credit card to be accepted when he texted back.

A what?

Tika smiled, picturing the way he had likely furrowed his brow and cocked his head as he read her message.

Sam leaned close and read over her shoulder. "Tell him it was probably black, about the size of a shoe box, and should have had lights on to verify connection. If he's not into computers, he probably mistook it as a regular part of her setup."

"He's not," she said, texting Sam's input to Wade. "He's into bugs and chemistry."

"Bugs?"

Tika glanced at her. "He's a science teacher."

"You guys and your love of nerds," Sam said, commenting on Eva's boyfriend Josh and all his useless science knowledge. She thanked the cashier and accepted the bagged dress while Tika put her wallet away.

As they walked out of the store, Tika's phone rang and she smiled, knowing it would be Wade. "Hello?"

"So," he said. "You couldn't have figured this out a week ago, huh?"

His voice was light and teasing, but she scrunched up her nose and said, "I know. I'm so sorry."

"No worries. The movers are almost done clearing out Lisa's place, but if you can meet me at the storage unit, we can start looking through boxes. I think I saw what you're talking about when I packed up her bedroom."

Tika unlocked her car and waited for Sam to get in, wanting a moment to speak to Wade freely, but Sam stood with a stupid grin on her face.

In response, Tika turned her back on her friend. "Are you doing okay?"

"I am," Wade responded. "I'm holding up surprisingly well."

"Is anyone there with you?"

"No. I'm good, Tika. This is the last part of clearing out her apartment that I have to take on alone."

"You're not alone," she said and then closed her eyes tightly because that sounded so damn cliché. "I just mean—"

"I know what you mean. Thank you for that." The tenderness and appreciation in his voice eased her embarrassment. "I really needed to hear that right now."

Her tense shoulders relaxed, and she let the crease between her brows soften. "If you text me the address for the storage unit, I'll meet you there, and we'll see if we can find this personal cloud thing."

"Personal cloud thing," he said, and she could easily picture his smile. "I'm not sure that's the technical term, but let's go with it. I'll see you there."

She put her phone back into her purse before turning around. The rainbows in her heart instantly faded when she spotted the smirk on Sam's lips.

"Shut up."

Sam laughed. "I didn't say anything."

"Get in the car, Sam, before I leave your ass here."

Tika ignored the obnoxious laugh that left her friend as she climbed into her car.

WADE SAT IN THE SAME CHAIR HE HAD OCCUPIED THE first time he had visited the HEARTS office. Just like that day, he felt as if someone was squeezing his chest so hard he could barely breathe. This time, though, when he glanced at Tika, he was able to push through the anxiety and remind himself to inhale. Exhale. And repeat. He knew it wasn't smart to count on her for emotional support, but he couldn't seem to help himself.

He was probably setting himself up for heartbreak. Though he thought she had the same attraction for him, he couldn't picture her intermingling business and pleasure. That disappointed him on so many levels, but he respected her too much to push. However, he would allow himself whatever comfort he could take right now, and looking at Tika was as close to comfort as he could get.

"Are you sure you want to be here for this?" Tika asked him just above a whisper.

He nodded as he looked at the big screen where Sam was projecting the content from her laptop. Sam glanced at him, as if verifying, and then she started scrolling through the files that Lisa had saved to the personal cloud drive.

Wade, Tika, and Sam had found the server after a few hours of opening boxes and sorting through the contents. They probably could have found it faster if Wade hadn't kept stopping to look at Tika and pretending Sam hadn't noticed. Tika had definitely looked beautiful, but he had come to realize his procrastination had nothing to do with Tika and everything to do with the fear of what they might find on the server.

Even so, they hadn't stopped searching until Wade finally lifted it out of a box and held it up as if he'd just found the Holy Grail. Sam had confirmed he'd found what they were looking for, then informed Tika she was owed drinks for the hours of time she'd put in.

"This could take a while," Sam said as she used her mouse to scroll over the many folders on the server. "Any idea where I should start?"

"Erin Diaz," Tika said.

Wade opened his mouth but then closed it. He needed to let Tika do her job, even if he still disagreed that Lisa's ex-girl-friend could possibly have something to do with Lisa's death. He had to trust her. He'd hired her to find out what happened to Lisa. Disagreeing with her every step of the way was not going to help her figure this mess out.

Sam typed Erin's name into the search option, and the drive whirled to life as it started sorting through the many files. Several folders popped up, each one labeled with a month. "Someone was a little OCD," Sam muttered. She clicked on the first one and let out a low whistle as photo thumbnails of Erin dressed, barely, in sexy clothing started lining up. "Close your eyes, big brother."

"Sam," Tika chastised. "Close it."

"Are you sure? There could be more to this than border-line pornography. Oh, there's a video. What do ya say?" she asked teasingly. "Should I click on that?"

"Samantha," Tika whispered harshly.

Wade felt heat rush to his cheeks as he turned away from the images of his sister's ex dressed as a sexy French maid. "Well. They were consenting adults."

"I would hope so," Sam said wryly. "Otherwise, your sister was a bit of a perv."

Tika cleared her throat and gave a silent *behave yourself*

glare to her coworker. He knew that look because his mother used to give it to him when he was being obnoxious at family dinners. The memories of those dinners nearly brought a smile to his face, but then he remembered they'd never be the same again. Not without his sister there to snicker along with him.

Though the thought of his sister and Erin dressing up and making videos wasn't something he ever needed to know, he was happy that Lisa had found someone to do those things with. She may have blown her relationship with Erin, but for a while at least, they'd had the kind of trust and bond to do such things. That took a special kind of relationship, and Wade was glad his sister had that before she passed away.

He wondered if he'd ever have that. Up until now, his relationships had been surface level only. He'd never met someone he'd felt a deep connection with. At least not someone he had dated.

He forced the thought away and focused on Tika, who was looking at the screen and occasionally lifted a brow. When curiosity started getting to him, he put his hand to the side of his face, effectively blocking any chance he might glimpse whatever images were showing on the screen.

Instead, he focused on Tika. Her hair was pulled back in a bun, like the first day he had met her, but it had been down when she'd shown up at the storage unit. She'd pulled it back with a band as they started sorting boxes.

He hadn't exactly been put out when Sam came with her, but he had been looking forward to spending time alone with Tika. They had bonded in a strange way that he didn't want Sam to intrude on. However, having three people, including one who actually knew what they were looking for, had ended the search for Lisa's drive much faster.

"Move on, Sam," Tika stated firmly. A moment later, she looked over at Wade and gave him a slight nod to let him know that the images of her sister's sex life were gone.

He returned his focus to the screen and watched as Sam made quick work of going through what was left in Erin's folder, including notes on the story that had cost Erin her job. Wade frowned at the confirmation that Lisa had used Erin as a source without consent.

Tika cast him a quick glance and then said, "Check for Lawrence Butler."

Within seconds, another string of folders appeared. The first one contained notes and the final story Lisa had written on Butler and his campaign. Nothing new there. The next, however, had a text document with a list of questions, clearly Lisa's string of thoughts. She had made notes to herself to research more on the Butler's marriage and their personal finances. More interestingly, at least as far as Wade was concerned, was the final note: *Infidelity?*

Wade glanced at Tika when he read that final line. She glanced at him as well.

Had Lawrence been unfaithful to his wife? Lisa seemed to think so. She must have been looking for evidence to support that. Maybe she'd even found it.

But then the next page had another note—one that made even more sense—to research how his campaign was funded. She had to have been digging into that. That must have been what tipped off the watchdog group.

"She was definitely suspicious of this guy," Sam

commented. "There are a dozen folders here. I think you'll want to take some time to go through these more closely."

"What's in that folder titled *Recording*?" Tika asked.

The next file, dated just a week before Lisa's death, held an audio clip. Sam clicked on it, and a deep voice filled the room.

"If you run that article," the male voice said, "I swear to God you will *not* live to regret it."

Wade's stomach dropped, and his heart seemed to stop beating for a moment before pounding back into a fast rhythm. That's it. That had to be it. The threat that had Lisa so upset the last time he'd seen her. He turned wide eyes to Tika. She acknowledged what he was thinking with a slight nod.

"Go to the next file," Tika said.

There were more notes about his campaign financing, this time with bank records and transactions highlighted yellow.

Wade swallowed as he dared to turn his eyes to her. She looked guarded, as if she didn't want him to know what she was thinking.

"Move on," Tika said.

Sam clicked on a few things before letting out another of her whistles, making Wade focus on the board again. These photos weren't of someone's bedroom fantasies playing out. These were images of a younger Lawrence Butler living his best life at party after party, some with scantily clad women, some in costumes, and all of them with heavy drinking being evident.

"Looks like ol' Mr. Butler was quite the frat boy in his college days," Sam said.

She quickly moved through the photos in the file. By the clothing and hairstyles, Wade would have to guess those were taken decades ago, which seemed to fit since the man he had seen on the news story about Lawrence Butler was not much older than him. Butler had been a party animal, but that wasn't enough to bring down a political campaign or to warrant a threat to the journalist digging into the story.

But the next folder was notes about accusations of hazing. Though Lisa had asked around, there didn't seem to be enough to pin any bullying to Butler himself. The next file was public reports about the Butler campaign's donors Lisa seemed to have pulled off the Internet.

They all stared at the screen as Sam moved through the report, but there was nothing to indicate what Lisa was looking at specifically.

"I'll dig into that more later," Tika said. "Try Dylan Tyler."

Sam found another group of folders and opened the first. There was a copy of her college paper story, the one that had caused Tika so many problems and had resulted in Dylan dropping out of school.

The next folder contained a thread of emails. As they read through them, the air in the conference room grew heavy with tension. Dylan had made not one but multiple threats against Lisa. He was going to sue her, the school, and anyone else he could blame for the troubles he seemed to have after dropping out.

Though his emails varied in who he blamed for what he was going through, they all circled back to one common theme: If Lisa didn't retract her story publicly, Dylan Tyler was going to come after her. And she would regret it if he did.

"Come after her," Wade said. "Is that a viable threat?"

"Not really," Tika said.

"But Lawrence's phone message was," he pressed. "He literally said she would not live to regret looking into him."

Tika ran her finger over her lips several times before looking at him. "I listened to her voicemails, Wade. That message wasn't on her cell phone. We have to find the original recording so we can try to trace the number where it came from and who made the call."

He gestured to the screen. "Lawrence Butler. Obviously."

"Not obviously," she said. "Not yet. We have to find a way to trace it to him before we can blame him for anything. Especially with him being a public official. Sam, can you pull up a video of Butler giving a speech so we can compare the voices?"

Moments later, the screen filled with Lawrence Butler's smug face as he announced he would be running for congress. Then Sam went back to the audio recording.

They all listened intently as she went back one more time to Butler's speech.

"They're not the same," Tika said. "That's not him."

"It's a voice recording through a phone," Wade justified, not willing to so easily dismiss what he was certain to be true. "Of course it doesn't sound the same."

"It's not him," Tika said again. "Wade, the voices are too different. It's not him."

"Then it's one of his flunkies," he insisted. "Every politician has a herd of assholes they use to do their dirty work. Any one of them could have made this call."

Tika nodded, but the motion was passive, as if she were placating him. "We have to find out which one before we can accuse him—"

"How are we supposed to do that?" he snapped. Closing his eyes, he blew out his breath. "Tika, it's in the folder Lisa made for Lawrence Butler. She wouldn't have put it there if the call hadn't been about him."

"That's not proof," Tika said. "I'm sorry, Wade, but unless we find something undeniable to tie that call to Lawrence Butler, then it's only speculation. That's not enough."

Sinking back, he let out a long slow breath. She was right. Though he knew that, he didn't want to agree. He wanted it to be enough. He needed it to be enough.

"I'm sorry," she said again.

He shook his head. "No. You're right. So, let's keep digging. She must have evidence somewhere." He ignored the concerned glances that Tika and Sam shared. They might not be willing to believe the call had come from Butler, but Wade did.

[7]

The hotel ballroom wasn't as large as Tika had expected. For some reason, she'd imagined the award ceremony would be more like some Hollywood celebration with gold statues and a red carpet rolled out for the guests where they'd pause for photos.

Instead, the musty old room was filled with about twenty round tables with eight chairs crammed around each one. Cheap plastic table covers had been used, and the decorations were limited to equally as cheap paper centerpieces in the shape of typewriters with table numbers and ABC confetti.

Little gift bags had pens, pencils, and other inexpensive trinkets from area newspapers and small businesses. Gold-wrapped chocolate coins had been carelessly tossed on each tabletop along with other wrapped candies. At the front of the room stood a lectern where she assumed speeches would be given. They hadn't even splurged for a stage.

They'd had to dress up for this? It seemed to her that business casual would have been sufficient. The little blue dress she'd bought was definitely overkill for the setting.

"Well," Wade said from beside her, "I was expecting..."

"More," Tika finished for him.

He smirked. "Yeah. More." After looking at the ticket in his hand, he pointed toward a table near the front. "Table four. Right there."

As they approached the table, Wade awkwardly rushed around her and pulled out a chair. He gave her a bashful smile as she thanked him. As she sat, he eased her chair in, and Tika had to bite her lip so she didn't laugh. Not at him but because she had a bad case of butterflies like she were at prom instead of some awards dinner with a client.

He sat next to her and smiled again, and Tika recalled how her breath had caught in her throat when Wade had opened his apartment door wearing what appeared to be the same suit he'd worn the day he'd hired her. She couldn't deny that she had noticed how handsome he was that day, but seeing him tonight sent a wave of something better left unnamed through her.

He had shaved for the so-called formal event. The usual hint of dark hair on his face was gone. She suspected if she touched his cheek now, his skin would be warm and smooth. He had somehow managed to tame his dark hair, and when he gave her that sweet smile of his, she couldn't help but think he looked more like a successful businessman than a nerdy science teacher.

She couldn't decide which look she liked more. Both worked well on him.

I'm not going to jump his bones. I'm not going to jump his bones.

Tika could swear he was having the same thoughts. His gaze skimmed over her low neckline, and a slight smile curved his lips. If this were a date, she'd put her hand on his and lean close to give him a better view of her cleavage. She didn't need a pushup bra, she had more than enough to fill the dress, but Sam had insisted and Tika was incredibly thankful. So was Wade, obviously.

When he finally tore his gaze from her neckline, he met her eye and stared slightly, as if he'd realized he'd been caught. His tongue darted across his lips as he forced himself to look around. Pink touched his cheeks, and he cleared his throat.

"Uh. Would you like a drink? Or...something?"

She smiled. "No. I'm okay. How are you?"

He focused on her again and his eyes were wide. "Um. Okay. Why?"

Her grin widened. "You just seem...nervous."

After a moment of holding her stare, he laughed lightly and gestured around. "You know, I'm not much for these things. If it weren't for Lisa's nomination..." His smile faded, and Tika forgot all about teasing him. "Well, I wouldn't be here if she could be."

She did put her hand on his then, but not to torment him with the sexual undercurrents they were both feeling. She couldn't stop herself from trying to comfort him. "Hey," she said softly, "you're okay. You're going to get through this. I'm right here, ready to help however I can."

Wade returned his attention to her, and his eyes no longer

held the embarrassment of an uncertain man on his first date. He looked sad. The look was so familiar to her now. His eyes held so much sorrow whenever he thought of his sister.

"Thank you," he said sincerely. "Thank you for being here." He lowered his gaze for a moment before his smile returned. "And for wearing that dress. It's really...nice."

Tika smiled, letting him redirect them to lighter topics. She glanced down to where his gaze seemed to have become fixated. The hemline was high on her thighs. Too high. But she didn't pull it down.

"I'm glad you like it."

"I do. Very much," he added. He looked into her eyes again and nearly scorched her with the fire in them.

She lightly traced his collar and then straightened the knot of his tie. "You look nice too."

The chattering of people approaching their table made Tika sit back. She wasn't sure if she was happy about having company or not. If she and Wade kept tossing teasing glances at each other, this night was going to go in a completely different direction than she'd planned.

While some of her coworkers had crossed intimate lines with their clients, Tika didn't think that was a great idea. Especially since Wade was her first client. *Ever.* She should save that particular indiscretion for much later in her career. If she ever engaged in that indiscretion.

Tika smiled as a trio joined them. They introduced themselves as reporters from a local paper. Wade nodded as he greeted them, then put his hand to his chest. "I'm Wade Steele. This is Tika Brown."

"Which paper are you with?" the woman named Ali

asked.

"Actually," Wade said and shifted uncomfortably, "I'm here on behalf of my sister, Lisa Steele."

Tika knew the others at her table recognized Lisa's name by the way they all grew quiet and cast uncomfortable glances at each other.

"We are very sorry about your sister," Ali said.

Wade perked up. "You knew her?"

Again, there was an awkward silence before Ali forced a smile that was as fake as a three-dollar bill. "Oh, yes."

Tika swallowed at how bitter the woman's underlying tone was. Clearly she wasn't a fan of Lisa. Tika only hoped Ali had enough class to keep that to herself. Wade was so honored to be sitting there to represent his sister, even if this wasn't his favorite way to spend an evening. He was there for Lisa, and that was important to him. A shadow of fear crept up Tika's spine—worry that Ali was going to tell him what she clearly thought of his sister.

Wade leaned closer, clearly not picking up on the signals Ali was sending. It was obvious to Tika that the woman would rather not discuss Lisa, but Wade pressed.

"Did you ever work with her?"

Ali glanced at her coworkers. "Well...not exactly." Her smile returned, and she focused on Tika. "What a lovely dress. Where did you get that?"

Tika glanced at Wade and saw the confusion on his face. He had been shut down, and he didn't seem to understand why. Tika squeezed his hand again, hoping he'd let go of his intent to question the reporter. She didn't think he'd want to hear what Ali thought of his sister, so she told Ali about the little boutique where Sam loved to shop and asked about her dress.

Soon they were joined by three others, filling their table. The others clearly knew Ali and her coworkers and began talking about things that left Wade and Tika on the outside of the conversation, which Tika thought was for the best. Lisa didn't seem to have the admiration from her peers that she had from her little brother. She wished he could take a step back and realize that there was clearly a side to his sister that he didn't know.

Tika had seen it, as had Erin Diaz and Dylan Tyler, and so many others. Wade simply refused to accept that Lisa's ambition outweighed her ethics at times. Tika suspected being around her peers might finally help him start to see a different side to his sister, and her heart ached for him. When —*if*—his blinders were ripped off, he was going to be heartbroken. Lisa's true colors weren't as bright and happy as Wade continued to believe, and when he realized that, he was going to have a hard time accepting his new reality.

"If you didn't work with her, how did you know her?" he asked. "Where did you meet her?"

Ali froze. So did her smile. She darted her eyes to Tika in what appeared to be a silent plea for help.

"Well," Ali stammered, "I didn't actually know her. Her reputation preceded her, I guess you could say."

Wade sat taller. "She was great at her job."

Ali nodded. "Yes."

The man next to her cleared his throat and sat forward. "What do you do, Wade?"

The air around the table became less tense when he said

he was a teacher, and the group at the table immediately started questioning him about the local school board and proposed budget cuts. Though the topic had been changed, Tika feared Wade would steer it back to Lisa at any time.

She was thankful when dinner was served and the focus around the table shifted to food. However, she could feel the tension mounting inside Wade. He was radiating stress, and she was concerned he might lose his hold on his composure. He wasn't an idiot. He'd noticed the uncomfortable reactions to Lisa's name as much as Tika had.

With food in front of them, the conversation faded and their group focused on the roasted chicken, steamed vegetables, and mashed potatoes. Again, Tika was grateful for the distraction.

Finally, the awards ceremony started. As with any ceremony like this, there were plenty of flat jokes that elicited kind laughter, a few stories that garnered actual laughs, and heartwarming stories. Soon enough, it was time for the presentation for *Best Freelance Exposé of the Year*.

Tika's stomach twisted into an unexpected ball of nerves. She didn't care if Lisa won for Lisa's sake, but she wanted Lisa to win for Wade. She wanted him to have this last moment of pride for his sister. This was more important to him than he tried to let on, but she could see through his attempts at being casual.

Without considering what she was doing, she grabbed his hand when the man behind the lectern began announcing nominees. Squeezing tight, she held her breath and waited.

"And the winner is," the local radio show host announced with flair, "Lisa Steele!"

The room filled with unenthusiastic applause. Tika looked around, trying to catch anyone other than Wade who was genuinely happy about the announcement. Those who were paying attention didn't seem excited. Several even looked upset. She hoped Wade wouldn't notice.

"Unfortunately," the speaker continued, "Lisa passed away earlier this year. Her award will be accepted by her brother, Wade."

Tika smiled at him, doing her best to be genuinely excited. The happiness in his eyes was undeniable, and she didn't want to take away from his moment. She knew that he was looking forward to taking this award to his parents and sharing this last achievement with them. She didn't want that ruined by the way the crowd was reacting, so she did her best to overcompensate for the lack of enthusiasm in the room.

"She won," he said as he beamed brightly at Tika.

"I'm so happy. Go," she encouraged. "Get her award."

He stood, seemingly oblivious to the underlying current of resentment in the room. At the lectern, he accepted the pen-shaped award and cleared his throat. Though no one else seemed pleased, the crowd was kind enough to grow quiet and let him have this moment.

"Um," he said and then glanced at Tika. "Thank you all for this award. My sister was my hero in so many ways. From the time we were kids, Lisa stood up for people. She never liked seeing the little guy getting pushed around."

"Whatever," someone at the table behind Tika said.

She stiffened. There was no logical way that Wade could have heard the comment, but her heart dropped to the pit of her stomach anyway. She glanced over her shoulder and narrowed her eyes at the woman who had the sense to look embarrassed that she'd been heard.

"I know my sister wasn't perfect," he said softly. "I know she made mistakes, but I loved her and I was proud of her. And"—he looked at the award in his hand—"I'm glad I can be here to accept this on her behalf. Thank you."

Soft applause filled the room, sounding only slightly more heartfelt than when Lisa's name had been announced, as he started back toward the table. He was about halfway back to his seat when a woman jumped up from a table as he passed her. Several people tried to stop her, but she made it to Wade before anyone could reach her.

Tika's smile fell when the woman grabbed his arm and jerked him to a stop. The look on her face was blatant anger. Tika rushed toward him and pushed the woman back several steps, instinctively shifting into self-defense mode. All the training HEARTS had put her through came rushing in a blur like a movie in fast forward. She put one leg slightly behind the other to shift her weight in case she had to defend herself or her client. Never mind that she was in a far too tight dress and shoes that could be considered weapons themselves.

If she actually had to defend Wade or herself, she wasn't going to have much luck. She'd likely break an ankle and flash the room before she was able to put a stop to this woman's attack. Even so, she made it clear to the woman that she wasn't going to grab Wade like that and get away with it.

The woman was only off balance for a few seconds before she found her footing and returned her hard stare toward Wade, or toward the award in his hands, to be more specific.

"She didn't deserve that," the woman seethed.

"Excuse me?" Wade asked.

The woman reached for the award in Wade's hands, but he pulled it back and up, out of her grasp as Tika once again gave her a slight shove, keeping her away from her client. The woman tried again, but Tika shoved again, harder this time, and the men behind the woman gently pulled her back.

"Lisa wasn't some heroic voice for the underdog," the woman stated, her accusation slurred. "She stole that story from me. She lied to me to get me to tell her what I knew."

Big surprise, Tika thought but then chastised herself. She had to stop casting judgment on Lisa. She was there for Wade, who was looking increasingly upset at the moment. No matter what Lisa had or hadn't done, this final proud moment he had for his sister was being ruined. Taken from him. And that made Tika's heart hurt.

She eased forward, just enough to draw the woman's attention. "Right now isn't the time for—"

"She was my mentor," the woman stated, glaring at Wade as if he were to blame. "I asked her to teach me how to earn a living being a freelance journalist because I looked up to her. I trusted her. I trusted her with my work and my career, and she betrayed me. I told her I had a lead, and I needed someone to help me. To teach me. And she stole that story from me." Once again, she turned her attention to the award in Wade's hands, looking at it with the longing of a starving puppy. Finally, she shook her head and tearfully said, "That should be mine."

"Sheryl," one of the men holding on to her said. "There will be other awards. Let this one go."

With a firm shake of her head, the fire returned to the woman's eyes. "I'm glad she's dead," Sheryl snarled. "She was cold-hearted and cruel, and I'm glad she's dead."

With the men holding onto Sheryl, Tika relaxed her defensive posture and turned to Wade. She put her hand on his arm, watching as his face melted from the shock of Sheryl's words.

"She's drunk," Tika whispered, but that did little to soften the hurt in his eyes.

"This isn't true," Wade responded just as softly. "None of it. It can't be. Lisa wouldn't..." The fact that his words trailed off instead of going down the road of denial he usually traveled confirmed Tika's fears. This was the night, the event, the moment when his rose-colored glasses came off and he started seeing the real Lisa Steele.

As she tried to calm Wade, the man behind Sheryl tried to hush her. When the woman was calmer, Tika turned her attention back to Sheryl. "Did you ever confront Lisa about stealing your story?"

Sheryl hesitated, as if unsure how to answer, like she hadn't expected anyone to take her accusation seriously. "I sent her texts."

Tika didn't recall seeing any texts accusing Lisa of stealing a story. In fact, she didn't even recall seeing Sheryl's name in Lisa's contacts. "How did she respond?" Tika asked, though she suspected she already knew.

"She said she thought the story I brought to her was a tip, not that I wanted to write it. That was a lie," Sheryl insisted. She looked from Tika to Wade to the men beside her. "That was a complete lie. I was very clear that I had a story that my boss wouldn't touch because he was scared of going up against one of his advertisers. Lisa had told me several times that she'd teach me how to get a story like that into papers without working for one. She said she'd teach me how to free-lance, all I had to do was find a big enough story. Which I did. I trusted her with my information, and she stole it from me. She *knew* that was my story." A big tear fell down Sheryl's cheek. "I gave up everything because I trusted her, and she used me to further her own career."

Wade opened his mouth, but Tika put her hand on his arm. "Did you see her after she released the story? Did you ever say all this to her face?" Tika asked.

Sheryl shook her head. "No. I couldn't. She stopped taking my calls and blocked me on social media. I couldn't get to her."

"Well," Tika asked and shrugged lightly, "did you ever try to corner her at her home or anything like that?"

Sheryl shook her head. "No. I was mad, but I'm not crazy." She shrank back a little as if she realized her actions contradicted that statement. "I was pissed, but I wasn't going to get arrested over this, and I have no doubt she would have tried that to keep me quiet. But I sure as hell am not about to let her get that award without making sure everyone knows how she got it." The anger and resentment returned to her slurred voice. She looked around the room and made sure everyone was looking at her. "She stole that story from me. That award was mine."

"Well, you did what you set out to do," the man who had tried to calm her said. "So, let's sit back down."

"Come on," Tika said softly before Wade could respond.

"There's no reason for us to stay any longer, Wade," she said when he didn't move. With a gentle nudge, she turned him toward the door. "It's time for us to call it a night."

The muscles in his jaw worked as his cheeks flushed a deep red. The shade spoke of his anger rather than the attractive blush that had found him earlier. He was furious, and Tika didn't blame him. Whatever Lisa might have done, that Sheryl woman was out of line attacking Wade like that and in front of all her peers.

Tika didn't think Sheryl had anything to do with whatever happened to Lisa. Even so, she peeked at the woman's name tag one more time. *Sheryl Hunter, Freelance Journalist/Photographer.*

Tika committed the name to memory so she could question the woman again. When she was sober and less confrontational.

THE HOTEL BAR WAS CROWDED, BUT WADE SPOTTED AN empty table and led Tika by the hand through the groups of laughing businesspeople and cozy couples. Dropping into a chair, he looked at her with desperation.

"What the hell just happened?"

The sympathy on her face made him cringe. Shaking his head, he dismissed her thoughts before she could share them.

"She's wrong," Wade insisted. "Lisa wouldn't..." He couldn't bring himself to finish his protest. Everywhere he turned these days, there was someone telling him that his sister wasn't the woman he'd thought her to be. He and his parents seemed to be the only ones who could see good in her. Everyone else insisted she was a liar, a manipulator, and now a thief.

He refused to buy into this version of her, but... How long could he tell himself that everyone else was wrong before he had to consider that he was the one who didn't know the real version of Lisa Steele?

Tika waved at a server and ordered two whiskeys. He didn't really want the drink, but he didn't refuse it either. His mind was a whirlwind. A hurricane. That woman had confronted him in front of an entire room of Lisa's peers, and not a single one stood up and defended his sister. Not one.

Raking his hand over his hair, he looked at Tika again. "She wouldn't do that. Would she?"

Tika frowned at him. "Honey, I think she would," she said softly.

Honey. She'd called him honey. But not in a term-of-endearment kind of way. Not in a way that made him feel special. It was a condescending term meant to soften the blow of the rest of her words. Wade didn't know if he should be pleased or pissed.

"Can't you at least pretend to be surprised?" he grumbled as the server slid a glass in front of him. Before he could take out his wallet, Tika handed some cash to the server, and she rushed off to fill the next order.

"Wade—"

He waved his hand to dismiss whatever Tika wanted to say. "Don't bother." After taking a drink, he let out a long breath to ease the burn of the whiskey. "She was my sister, Tika. No matter what she did, she was my sister."

"Wade," she said softly as she put her hand on his arm. "I know that. No one wants to take her away from you."

"Just tarnish her memory, huh?" he asked with more accusation than he'd intended.

She was quiet for several long, heavy seconds before saying, "You have to face the fact that Lisa was not the person you thought she was."

"Don't start," he warned through clenched teeth.

"I'm not saying she was a bad person," Tika continued. "We all make mistakes. We all make bad choices sometimes."

"Yeah. You're making one right now," he barked.

She sank back, taking her hand with her, and he immediately regretted snapping.

"Sorry, I..." Closing his eyes, he pressed his fingertips to the bridge of his nose and exhaled slowly. "She was my sister," he said again.

"That doesn't make her perfect."

Dropping his hand onto the table, he eyed her. He didn't know what to say. Because she was right, and as much as he hated it, he was starting to question his view of Lisa. "I can't believe she did these things. I refuse to."

"I see that," she said with a voice that was void of the warmth she'd been offering him just moments before, "but refusing to believe something doesn't make it any less real. A science teacher should know that."

He laughed slightly. "Dragging science into this? That was unexpected."

Tika's stiff posture softened, and she gave him a hint of a sympathetic smile. "Stop basing your results on your feelings and start looking at the evidence, Wade. All these people are telling you the same thing. This isn't some wild conspiracy to tarnish her memory. The entire world didn't wake up one day and decide on the same narrative to share. Nobody sent out a memo with talking points. Whether you want to believe it or not, your sister used people to get to where she was."

He opened his mouth to disagree, but he couldn't find a logical argument to give her. She was right. Lisa had disclosed Tika's name. She had wrongfully implied Dylan Tyler was engaging in racist behavior. She'd used Erin's private conversation to get a lead. And, apparently, she'd stolen Sheryl Hunter's story. A knot formed in his stomach, turning it upside down until it ached. His heart pounded, and sadness filled his soul.

"I'm not saying she was a bad person," Tika continued more gently. "A lot of people get caught up in building their careers and don't realize they are hurting others along the way, but she *did* hurt people, Wade. And if you're right and someone was responsible for her death, it was probably someone she crossed. Maybe it's time to rethink your decision to look into what happened to her."

He started shaking his head before she even finished speaking. "I am more convinced than ever that someone hurt her. I don't care if they are right. I don't care if she clawed her way to every story she ever wrote. That doesn't change what she meant to me." He pointed to his chest and swallowed when his voice cracked. "She will always be my big sister. I will always love her. The list of people who could have done this just keeps growing, right? That means the odds keep turning against this being an accident. Okay, so she screwed someone over. She crossed the wrong person. That person still killed her, Tika. That person still took her life. I want that person found. I want that person to pay for taking her from me. From our parents."

She frowned. "Okay. Then we'll keep looking."

"Yes. We *will* keep looking."

"Even though you know you may keep finding things you don't like," she said with a gentle voice.

In a strange way, the fact that he was starting to realize that he didn't know his sister as well as he thought he did made him more determined. He might not like what she did, but no one was perfect, right? No one made the right decisions all the time. This was a side of Lisa that she hid away from him. He didn't like this part of her, but he wanted to know all he could. Because the reality was, he'd probably never get another chance to know her—all of her—before the memory of her started fading.

"Nothing is going to make me love her less." Taking Tika's hand, he clung to her as he stared into her dark eyes. "You'll help me?"

She nodded. "Yes. Of course, I'll help you."

"Good." Relief washed away some of the darkness that had settled over him. "Because I tried to do this on my own, and I don't know what the fuck I'm doing."

Tika laughed as she tightened her hold on his hand. "I'm happy to help, Wade. But I'm not going to lie to you about what I find. Even if you don't like it."

The edge of his anger slipped away. Her dedication to being honest had pissed him off more than once, but he did appreciate that about her. He appreciated that she didn't sugarcoat or lie to placate him. That wouldn't help this situation. In fact, it would be worse when he did discover the truth.

"Thank you for standing by me, Tika. I don't think you realize how much this means to me. I know you didn't really want to take on this case. I'm starting to finally understand why."

Tika held on to his hands when he started to pull away. When he looked at her, she held his gaze. "I want you to know that I understand where you are coming from. No matter what decisions Lisa made in her career, she was still your sister. She still stood up to the neighborhood bully for you, right?"

He smiled, remembering the story he'd told her of the kid who always stole his toys. Even now he could hear his sister screaming at the bully to leave her brother alone. The memory faded, and he pictured this newer version of his sister —the woman who would seemingly do anything for a story.

The sadness in his heart must have shown on his face, because Tika cupped his cheek and lightly brushed her thumb over his skin. When he looked up at her, she offered him a smile.

"If someone hurt her," she whispered, "I'll find out. I promise."

Covering her hand, he nodded. "I believe you."

[8]

Tɪᴋᴀ ᴇʏᴇᴅ the letterboard as she walked into the DeLanka Hotel downtown. The board announced that Lawrence Butler would be there later that evening and gave a list of rooms and times for events.

Every time Tika turned around these days, that man was right there in her face. She supposed it was one of those psychological tricks Rene liked to ramble about. Like as soon as someone decides to buy a sky-blue car, they see sky-blue cars everywhere. Association, or something like that.

Tika wasn't here to see Lawrence Butler or attend his event, however. According to Sam, Dylan Tyler was working security at the DeLanka and could likely be found in a small office tucked away down a long hall on the first floor. All Tika had to do was get there.

Easy-peasy, cute butt squeezy, Sam had said.

"Easy-peasy, my ass," Tika muttered.

During the morning meeting at HEARTS, she'd told her team that her plan for the day was to interview Dylan

Tyler about the threats he'd made toward Lisa. She wasn't confident that had been his voice on the voicemail, but she had to try to get a voice recording of him so she could compare the voices next to each other. Dylan made the most sense in Tika's mind. As soon as she'd shared her intentions, her teammates had rattled off suggestions and advice, and Sam had started digging into the layout of the hotel and was able to identify where the security office should be.

By the time Tika had left HEARTS, she felt equally prepared for the interview and terrified by the advice she'd been given.

Rolling her shoulders back, she took long strides as she headed for the hallway. She was nearing where the office should have been according to the signs on the wall, when someone called out to her.

"Miss," a man said.

Tika stopped and turned, forcing a soft smile to her lips as she put her hand to her chest. "Me?"

"Do you have an appointment or something?"

Her stomach knotted around itself. Confrontation. Her biggest weakness. She hated confrontation. Every drop of liquid in her mouth seemed to have evaporated at once.

What would Holly do?

She wouldn't freeze and stand there with doe eyes. That was for certain.

Tika forced her smile to widen as she stood even taller. "I work with Lawrence Butler's team," she said without hesitation. "I'm here to check on a few things with security before tonight's event."

The man hesitated, as if mentally testing the validity of her story.

"I was told to speak with Dylan Tyler." Tika swallowed as soon as that lie slipped from her lips. That might have been a step too far. That might have tipped the scales against her.

The man nodded. "Ah." He pointed down the hall. "Third door on the right."

She nodded stiffly, not quite believing she hadn't been caught sneaking through the business offices of the hotel. Especially hours before a political event. Granted, Lawrence Butler was still a relatively unknown candidate outside of his district, but she would have thought there would be better security surrounding his event.

Turning, she let out her breath slowly as she forced herself to walk confidently toward her destination. She didn't know if the man was still watching, and she didn't want to glance back on the off chance that'd make him suspicious, but she made herself walk as if she were supposed to be there.

"Feeling nervous is fine. Expected even," Rene had once told her while training Tika for moments just like this, "but if you look nervous, you'll draw attention to yourself."

Tika stopped at the door marked as the security office and ran another piece of Rene's advice through her mind. *Remember to keep your shoulders back, your chin up, and to make eye contact as you smile.*

Tika fumbled with her phone to get the recording option ready to go. She wanted to be recording when she walked into the room. Then if he told her she couldn't record him, she'd still have a sample to compare to Lisa's voicemail.

"On the count of three," Tika whispered to herself as she

tapped the icon on her phone to start the recording. However, she only counted to one before opening the door and plastering a smile on her face. As soon as he walked in, she was met with curious brown eyes and a perplexed look that brought back some unexpected feelings.

Dylan Tyler. All-American jock-type. The type of guy who people used to listen to, back when he was admired. The kind of guy who could have told a fellow jock to shut the hell up and he would have been listened to. His stance would have been respected.

Instead, he'd stood next to Tika with that same stupid look on his face as he watched her being bullied. He'd stood back and said nothing. Done nothing.

In that moment, she didn't feel the least bit sorry that Lisa's story had undermined his life goals. In that moment, seeing him sitting there in a security uniform with a bright-yellow logo on his chest instead of an expensive suit made her appreciate Lisa for the first time in a very long time.

Lisa had disrupted Tika's life, but she'd brought this jerk to his knees. His big life plans certainly hadn't include sitting at a desk in a cheap uniform looking at monitors all day.

"Tika Brown," he said softly as he sank back in his chair. "What the hell are you doing here?"

Tika glanced around the room. There were two other people sitting at similar desks, but as soon as they saw Dylan greet her, they went back to whatever they were doing. Nobody was paying any attention to the two of them. That was good, she supposed.

Don't forget to assess the room. That had been Alexa's advice. Know what you're walking into.

Tika skimmed the area, finding a door that she could rush through if the need arose. She didn't think it would. Not with other people in the room. Worst case scenario: Dylan got pissed and threw her out. She didn't think he'd elevate that to any kind of physical altercation where she'd need an escape route.

"I actually came looking for you," Tika said. Though she had elephants rolling around in her stomach, she was pleased that her voice came out confident and strong.

The perplexed look on his face turned into a frown. "Why?"

"Do you remember Lisa Steele?"

He jolted. The widening of his eyes said a thousand things, and she was trying to decipher each one. Surprised. Taken aback. He recovered quickly, blinking and clearing his throat before blowing out a breath. "Hard to forget the person responsible for your life going to shit."

"Yeah," Tika said lightly. "It is. She certainly screwed up my life plans." Camaraderie was a great way to get people talking. If there was one thing Tika had in common with Dylan, it was that their lives had been upended after Lisa's article hit the press.

His stiff posture relaxed a little. "Mine too. I guess you heard she bit the big one."

Bit the big one? That was a nice way to say she'd died. "Yeah," Tika said without commenting how that was a fairly crass observation.

"I, um..." Dylan sighed and met Tika's gaze. "I'm sorry. About what happened back in college. Lisa screwed up my life by implying that I was discriminating against my classmates, but she was right in saying that I should have stood up when I saw bad shit happening. I saw that guy treating you like crap at a party, and I didn't say anything. I should have. I'm sorry about that, Tika."

She considered his emails, the ones where he called her a bitch and threatened to force her to tell the world he hadn't taken part in the harassment that had upended all their lives. Instead of pointing out that he didn't seem especially remorseful, she recognized those comments had likely been made in anger. She simply nodded and opted to let them go.

"Thanks. Apology accepted."

He offered a slight smile. "Good, because I've felt bad about that for a long time." He tilted his head to the right a bit. "So. What are you doing here?"

"Lisa's brother doesn't think her death was an accident."

As soon as the words left her, Dylan's face changed. His jaw set and his eyes turned hard. The air around them filled with electricity. Dylan's demeanor instantly stiffened as if preparing to pounce on Tika if needed.

"You threatened her several times," Tika added.

"Are you a cop?"

"Private investigator."

A snide smirk twisted his lips. "Are you fucking kidding me?" he muttered. "And this is what you're looking into? Lisa fucking Steele's death?"

"Her brother hired me."

"Why would he hire you?"

She didn't want to get into Wade's misguided reasons. "Because I'm good at what I do, and if there was more to Lisa's death than an accident," she said in a cocky tone she'd heard her more established coworkers use in interrogation a hundred times, "I'll find a way to prove it."

He shifted in his seat and gave his head a slight shake. "I don't have to talk to you if you aren't a cop."

"You don't, but you should. Is it okay if I record this?" she asked in an intentionally rushed voice while waving her phone. "You made quite a few threats toward Lisa before her untimely death. You can talk to me, or I can hand over the evidence I have to the police."

Stiffening, Dylan met Tika's gaze. "No, you can't record this."

She tapped her phone to end the recording and then put the phone back into her purse.

He waited until the device was out of sight before asking, "Are you accusing me of something?"

She shrugged. "I'm stating facts. We have emails and a voicemail."

"I never left her a voicemail," he stated firmly. "*Never.* I didn't even have her phone number. I got her email off all those stories she was publishing, but I never got her number."

Tika lifted her brows to imply she didn't believe him. She'd listened to the voicemail enough to know it wasn't his voice, but he didn't know that. "Dylan," she practically cooed. "You were furious with Lisa. You said she'd ruined your life."

"She did."

"You said if she didn't print a retraction, you were going to get her."

"Sue her," he clarified. "I said I'd *sue* her. There's a big difference between killing someone and suing someone. If you're so great at your job, you'd know that. Then again," he said and offered her a cruel smirk, "you did have to drop out of law school because of her, didn't you?"

She simply smiled instead of replying. "I'll tell you what I know," Tika pressed. "You blamed Lisa for your inability to get a job."

He held his hands out. "What do you call this?"

She made a show of looking around at monitors keeping tabs on virtually every corner of the hotel. "I call this a far cry from the political aspirations you droned on and on about in college."

His face reddened as the muscles in his jaw worked. She'd hit the right button with that. He was about to lose control and have one of those emotional outbursts that tended to reveal someone's true colors. She held her breath, waiting. Anticipating.

But after about five intense seconds, he scoffed and sat back. He'd put a lid on his temper before losing it, almost as if he realized she'd been waiting for that moment to see just how violent he could become. Instead, he sank into his chair and smirked at her.

Damn it.

"Do you have some kind of warrant or something that says I have to talk to you?"

"No."

"Then I guess you better go."

"You can talk to me, or you can talk to the police. It won't be long before they start digging into those emails, Dylan."

He seemed to consider her warning for a few seconds before discounting the words and nodding toward the door. "Go. I'm done talking to you."

Tika hesitated before turning away.

"Hey," Dylan called as she neared the door. When she faced him again, he said, "She never changed. You should know that. She was still the same liar and manipulator that she'd been in college."

"I've heard."

"So maybe she got what was coming to her."

Tika lifted her brow. "Interesting thought, Dylan. But I don't think her brother or her grieving parents would agree."

She had heard the other investigators at HEARTS talking about how their guts talked to them. She understood what they meant now. Dylan was hiding something, but Tika didn't know what, and she didn't know how to pry it out of him. But there was something here. Something more that she couldn't pinpoint.

She would have to hash it out with one of her coworkers later. If she pressed now, she suspected Dylan would make a scene and throw her out. Smiling warmly at him, she batted her eyes.

"It was wonderful seeing you, Dylan. Congratulations on finally finding gainful employment."

He grunted in response and returned his attention to the screens.

Tika left him and the hotel. As soon as she was in her car, she called Sam.

"What's up?" Sam asked as a greeting.

"Did you find Sheryl Hunter?"

"Of course. I'll text you her address."

"Where's she working?"

"Freelance, from what I can tell. She gave up working for

someone else about eight months ago and listed herself as a freelance journalist."

"Do me a favor," Tika said but didn't want Sam to agree before continuing. "Sheryl claimed Lisa stole the story she won an award for last night. The story was titled something like 'Sexual Harassment: A Staple of Big Business.'"

"Found it," Sam said moments after Tika finished speaking.

"When was that released?"

Sam harrumphed. "Seven months ago."

"One month after Sheryl gave up everything to freelance."

"How long does it take to research and write an exposé like that?" Sam asked.

Tika blew out her breath. "About a month or so, I'd guess."

"What a bitch," Sam muttered.

Tika didn't have the words to argue. It certainly seemed like Sheryl was telling the truth. Lisa had stolen her story. Of course, there was no way to hear Lisa's side of things, and Tika couldn't very well argue that with Wade.

"You texted me her address?"

"Yup."

"I'm headed that way, then."

"Be safe," Sam said.

"Always." She ended the call and checked the text, thankful that Sheryl's apartment wasn't too far from Wade's house. Within fifteen minutes, she was knocking on Sheryl's door. Shuffling on the other side let her know that someone was there, and a moment later, the door opened.

The woman from the night before—looking hungover—cracked the door and peered out. She frowned and heaved a sigh.

"I just want to ask you a few questions," Tika said.

"I shouldn't have done what I did," Sheryl said, her voice dry and cracked.

"I understand why you did."

Her words clearly surprised Sheryl, who opened the door and let her in. "I was upset."

"I know."

"Don't mind the mess. I'm not much of a housekeeper."

Tika offered her a soft smile as she walked in. She scanned the room, as she'd been taught to do, and her heart skipped a beat when she spotted a camera sitting on the table. The model looked exactly like the one Wade insisted was missing from Lisa's belongings. Tika's heart started pounding.

Holy shit. Ho-ly. Shit.

"Want something to drink?" Sheryl offered.

"Uh, no." Tika tore her gaze from the camera and smiled at Sheryl again. "Thank you."

"Look," Sheryl said, sagging in the oversized T-shirt she wore. "I'm sorry I lashed out at your boyfriend like that."

"He's not my boyfriend," Tika said. She reached into her back pocket and pulled out a business card to give to Sheryl. "I'm a private investigator. Lisa's family has cause to believe her death wasn't accidental."

Sheryl looked at the card and frowned. "Look, I hated that backstabbing bitch, but I didn't kill her."

"Oh, I know that," Tika said with a forced laugh. "I just

wanted to know who else Lisa might have slighted. I'm sure the list is long."

Sheryl scoffed. "Yeah. Her brother's speech was nice, but he's wrong about her. She would have thrown his ass in front of a bus to get a story."

Tika didn't even have the urge to argue. That was the side of Lisa that she knew too. She wished she could put that idea out of her mind, for Wade's sake, but the truth was too hard to ignore. Lisa was a user, a manipulator, and a backstabber. And Wade had wool over his eyes.

"Can you think of anyone who was angry enough to confront her?" Tika asked.

"Most of the journalists I knew just avoided her. They knew what she was like. A few even tried to warn me, but I considered her a friend, and I trusted her. I thought she was a mentor. I didn't..." Scoffing, Sheryl sank at the table where the camera was sitting.

Taking the opportunity, Tika sat next to her. "Great camera," she said and picked it up without asking. Turning it over, she found the serial number printed in small font. She had the number from Lisa's camera memorized. She'd read the file so many times. The numbers didn't match. This wasn't Lisa's camera.

"That was the kind Lisa used. I bought it because... Because I wanted to be like her," Sheryl said. "I was so blind. I was such a fool to trust her. I thought we were friends, but she just saw me as another rung on the ladder for her success. Nothing was sacred to her, not even friendship."

Easing the camera down, Tika nodded her understanding. "There are a lot of people like that in the world. Lisa wasn't alone in that."

"No, I suppose not." Sheryl toyed with the strap of her camera. "If you really think someone hurt her, you should look into the people she wrote about. She burned some journalists here and there, but she went for the jugular when she was doing her exposés. Many bright lights were extinguished at her hand. Politicians, businessmen—hell, even a few school board members had to resign by the time she got through with them. But she had her sights set high. She was looking to take down the big fish to make a name for herself. Anyone on her radar was in danger of being taken down."

One name immediately came to Tika's mind.

Lawrence Butler

A rising political star that Lisa had definitely taken notice of. And his wife had noticed. Had even warned Lisa to back off.

"What about this corporation she wrote about? The story she stole from you?"

Sheryl shook her head. "They wouldn't make threats. They'd just sue. Actually, I wouldn't be surprised if somewhere there was a lawsuit in the works. Most of her sources were anonymous, but one of them might have been upset enough to threaten her. But," she said thoughtfully, "most of her sources were women who were tired of being harassed, so I'm not sure why they'd make a fuss."

Sheryl rubbed her fingers against her temple. "Sorry. I'm not being much help."

"Actually," Tika said softly, "I think you've been more help than you realize." Standing, she thanked the woman and suggested she drink more water as she made a mental note to go back to those files. She was going to have to look into Lawrence Butler again. And more seriously this time.

Maybe Wade was right. Maybe someone on Butler's team did want Lisa to shut up enough to kill her.

WADE HISSED WHEN THE BAKING SHEET IN HIS HAND seared his fingertips. He dropped the sheet onto the stovetop and cursed under his breath.

"Wade?"

He jolted and turned around.

"Sorry," Tika said. "I didn't mean to startle you. I knocked, but you must not have heard me. You okay?"

"I burned my hand on the damn...thing."

Tika tilted her head. "Baking sheet."

"Yeah, that thing."

"Bad day?" she asked as he ran his hand under cold water.

"I guess you could say that," Wade seethed as he turned around. Noticing that the oven door was still open, he angrily brought his foot up and kicked it closed, causing Tika to jump as the crash filled her ears. "I'm so fucking sick of this."

"Hey," Tika said quietly. "Wade. Wade, fighting with the oven won't help. Sit down, come on, sit down and talk to me. What happened?"

Sitting at the table, he leaned forward and lowered his head while she cut the pizza that had cooled on the cookie sheet. He didn't even want the pizza. He'd needed a distraction. "I kept thinking about last night. Replaying that entire scene and how no one, not one single person stood up for Lisa."

Sliding a slice of pizza in front of him, Tika hovered close but didn't say anything.

Wade ground his teeth together. "She was... She was everything Sheryl accused her of being, wasn't she?"

Tika ran her hand over the back of his head and around his jaw until she could tilt his head up. "I'm so sorry, but I think so."

"She was my sister," he choked as his arms went around her waist, pulling her tightly against him.

She ran her fingers through his hair as he buried his head in her chest. "No matter what she did," Tika whispered, "she didn't deserve someone to hurt her. If someone did, I'll find out who."

He choked out a sob at her promise. He'd been wrestling with this unwanted truth all day. He'd been torn, but the truth was becoming too much to deny. Lisa wasn't the person he thought. He felt like he was losing his sister all over again, and it was breaking his heart.

Wade wasn't sure how long he had sat there, absorbed in her arms, letting his emotions finally escape him while she stroked his back and held his head against her, but it wasn't long enough, it would never be long enough. Nothing could take this pain away. Slowly leaning back, he eased his grip on her but didn't completely release her.

"I'm sorry. For what she did to you."

Tika slowly shook her head as she ran her hands over his hair again. "Don't ever apologize for something that someone else did. That was out of your control."

"I needed to hear that," he confessed quietly. "I don't know how I couldn't have seen through her."

She smiled softly as she leaned back to look at his face, gently putting a hand to his cheek, she dried what remained of his tears. "You loved her, Wade. She couldn't have been all bad."

"I should have seen through her. Maybe I could have helped her change before she crossed the wrong person."

"We don't know that something like that happened to her," Tika said, reminding him of something she'd been telling him from the day they'd met.

He managed a weak smile. "I know."

Begrudgingly, she stepped back and took his hand. "Come on."

Letting her lead him, Wade followed her into the living room and watched while he watched her clear the newspapers off the couch.

"Lie down," she ordered. "Want me to heat up your pizza?"

"No thanks."

"I can make you a sandwich."

Wade shook his head as he sat down heavily on the sofa. "Naw."

"Coffee, soda, tea?"

"Water?"

Tika smiled. "Water it is."

He watched her disappear before kicking his shoes off and stretching out on the couch. As he stared at the ceiling, he tried to convince himself she was right. They didn't know something nefarious had happened to Lisa. But he felt it. In his gut. Like she were whispering to his soul to find the person and prove she'd been killed. He supposed there was no way to convince Tika of that any more than she could seem to convince him that Lisa's death was an accident.

A few moments later, she reappeared, two water bottles in hand along with a bowl of grapes and gestured for him to scoot over. "What else happened today?"

Wade sighed as he rolled over onto his side to make room for her. "Just the usual. How about you?"

Sitting on the edge of the couch, she sipped her drink. "Well," she said thoughtfully as if debating what to say. "I talked to Dylan Tyler."

"And?"

She looked at her water bottle. "He wasn't exactly forthcoming with information. I think he's hiding something. I need to find a new way to go about questioning him."

Wade sat up slightly. "What do you think he's hiding?"

"I don't know. It could be something as simple as he didn't want to talk to me. He says he didn't leave that voicemail."

"Do you believe him?"

"He seemed sincerely surprised to hear about it. I think we have to consider it was someone else."

"Lawrence Butler. I'm telling you."

"Maybe. I'm not ruling him out." She glanced back at him. "I also talked to Sheryl. The journalist—"

"I know who you mean," he said, sounding more curt than he'd intended.

"She said if anyone hurt Lisa, it was probably someone she was investigating or someone recently targeted by one of her exposés."

Wade threw his hand in the air. "Lawrence Butler."

Tika set her water bottle on the end table. "We can't just accuse him of something, Wade. I have to find evidence."

"Question him."

She nodded. "I intend to."

"So let's go."

She put her hand to his chest to stop him from sitting up. "There's an event at a hotel tonight."

"Perfect."

"Not perfect," she informed him. "It's at the hotel where Dylan Tyler works."

"So you know exactly where it's at."

"I also know that it's going to be crawling with security, and we don't have tickets to get in. I'll find a way to corner Butler and ask him what he knows about your sister, but we aren't going to make a scene at a fundraising event."

When he dragged his hand over his face and let out a long breath, Tika frowned. He was exhausted. The dark circles and ashen complexion were testament to how tired this man had become in the last few weeks.

"I'm going to question him," Tika said. "But I can't until I have real questions to ask him, Wade. Not just speculation or accusations. I know this is frustrating, but you have to be patient."

"I know," he whispered. Dropping onto his sofa, he let out a long breath. "It's all a bit too much sometimes, you know?"

"I do know." She smiled softly. "When's the last time you slept more than a few hours?"

He smirked. "I don't even know what day it is, let alone when I last slept."

"Why don't you relax for a few, and I'll reheat your pizza?"

The words were barely out of her mouth before he leaned his head back and closed his eyes. He listened as she puttered in his kitchen. He didn't know why the sound was so soothing. She wasn't doing anything other than making noise, but for some reason that seemed right. Having her there, making herself at home, felt right. Comforting.

For the first time since seeing his sister lying in a hospital bed with wounds from which he knew she'd never recover, he felt the fist around his heart easing. He still hurt, he was still aching in a way he couldn't describe, but having Tika doing what she could to help him eased the pain.

He wanted more of that.

Hearing her come back into the living room, walking softly as if she were afraid to wake him, made him smile. Opening her eyes, he watched her ease the plate down and glance back.

"I thought you might be sleeping."

"No, not yet."

"You should eat this and then go to bed. I'll see you tomorrow."

Wade cleared his throat as she turned away. "Stay. Please."

When she hesitated, he gently gripped her hand. "Will you stay?" he asked sleepily.

"You need sleep."

He pulled at her, and she nearly fell onto him. A slight laugh left her as she sat on the edge of the sofa. "What are you doing?"

"Playing on your pity so you stay with me."

"Well, at least you're honest."

He softened his teasing smile and said, "I don't want to be alone. Stay with me."

Finally, she sat beside him. He put his arm around her shoulders and hugged her closer. "This is a terrible idea," she whispered.

Wade let out a slow breath as he nuzzled closer, burying his face in her hair. "Yeah, it is."

"You're feeling emotional," she said as she intertwined his fingers in hers.

"That's not what I'm feeling right now," he whispered. "I want you," he confessed.

"I know," she answered.

He smiled. "Is that an acknowledgment or a confession that you feel the same?"

"Both."

His heart very nearly jumped from his chest.

Looking up at him with her dark-brown eyes, she sighed. "I'm not sure we should do this, though. Not until after..."

He knew what she was saying. He understood why she felt that way, but as he traced his fingertips over her jawline, her words faded, and it seemed her conviction did as well. She sighed and sagged slightly, easing her rigid posture.

Wade's breath caught as she put her hand on his knee and squeezed. "I want to kiss you."

She was quiet for so long that he feared she didn't feel the same, but finally, she looked up at him and he could breathe again.

"So kiss me," she said as softly.

He leaned down and pressed his mouth to hers. The fear he had evaporated as she pressed her tongue against his lips, encouraging him to let her in. Feeling her return his kiss with as much heated passion as he was giving gave him all the encouragement he needed. Breaking the kiss, he searched her eyes for any doubts but found none. Guiding her with his body, he urged her to stretch out until she was beneath him.

He slid his hand down her side to her thigh and filled his fist with the soft material of her slacks. Tika turned her head, letting his lips move to her neck, where he gave her the same passionate treatment. Moving down her body, Wade cupped her breast through her blouse, roughly teasing her with his hot mouth through the thin barrier while his hand wrestled to pull the material from her waistband. Sighing when he finally felt her warm skin against his hand, he massaged her side as he lowered his kisses.

Tika moaned softly when he kissed the curve of her breast. Slipping her hands between them, she started unbuttoning her shirt, exposing a light-blue lace bra. Damn, he did love her in blue. As she sat enough to remove her shirt, he lifted his over his head, tossed it aside, and then went to work on her slacks.

Minutes later, he was in a pair of boxers, admiring the matching underwear she was still sporting.

"Condom," she whispered when he reached for what remained of her clothing.

Wade cursed. Condom. "Uh."

Tika smirked at him and fumbled for the purse that was sitting on the coffee table. Moments later, they were both somehow naked, and she was covering his erection. Her face seemed to mirror his, raw lust needing to be released, needing to go somewhere before it exploded. She leaned up and kissed him, gently biting his lip, tugging his mouth toward hers. Slipping his tongue in her mouth, he dueled with her momentarily before leaning back and looking at her face.

Wrapping her legs around his, she met each thrust with as much power. He didn't stop until he felt like his mind was separating from his body. Feeling her slowly start to relax around him, Wade groaned as he eased down, supporting himself so that he didn't crush her.

"Wow," he breathed.

She smiled. "Yeah."

[9]

Waking up next to Wade had been nice, but Tika had slipped out of his bed and rushed back to her apartment to shower before the sun peeked over the horizon. He'd woken enough to pull her to him for a kiss, but then he'd drifted back off to sleep.

As soon as his breathing returned to a deep, even pattern, she'd eased out of the bed, dressed, and rushed home. She didn't want to risk being late getting to work, and she hadn't packed for a sleepover.

From the moment she'd walked out of his house, she'd been filled with a mix of happiness and regret. Not regret, really...that was too strong a word. But she certainly wished she'd held off on having sex with him until after the case was solved. If she couldn't find the evidence Wade was so desperately craving, she had no idea what that would do to their relationship.

Would they even have a relationship if she had to tell him that Lisa fell? That was it. She fell. She suspected that was what this was going to come to, and she had no idea how he'd take that. He'd gone from blaming Lawrence Butler to Sheryl Hunter to Dylan Tyler. Whoever was convenient took the blame. Everyone was subject to suspicion, even if there wasn't sufficient evidence to support that suspicion.

He simply couldn't seem to accept that maybe Lisa slipped and fell. Maybe her camera wasn't stolen. Maybe it had been lost. Maybe he was putting himself through hell instead of accepting his loss and allowing himself to grieve. And the only thing he might get out of this is a tarnished version of his sister.

Tika tapped her pen on the conference room table, only stopping when Alexa swatted at her hand. "Sorry," Tika muttered and set the pen aside.

"You've been withdrawn since getting in this morning. What's bothering you?"

Shifting in her seat, Tika pushed away the flash of Wade kissing her passionately and forced her focus on her coworker. "Just trying to figure out what, if anything, happened the night Lisa fell."

"You're still not convinced someone pushed her?"

Tika debated how to answer that. She understood now why Wade was so convinced. There were so many people who seemed to be angry with Lisa. Any one of them could have given her a push without meaning to hurt her. Or could have intentionally thrown her to her death. Either way, whatever the motive, someone could have been upset enough to confront her. But she just couldn't prove anything, and without proof, how the hell was she supposed to find the person—if there was one—responsible?

"The only evidence Wade has that someone was involved in her death is that her camera is missing. However, there's no proof that she had her camera with her. This is all speculation, and I have to wonder if I'm doing him more harm than good by continuing to chase shadows when the reality is that she may have just slipped."

"Is he willing to accept that?"

"I don't think so. The thing is... The list of people who may have had a motive to hurt her is growing by the day. Literally by the day, Lex. And her camera is still missing," Tika said. "It hasn't shown up at any pawn shops or online sales sites that I can find. She was receiving death threats and harassing emails. Dylan Tyler says he never left Lisa a voicemail, and I actually believe that. I kind of sneaked a recording of his voice so I could compare them." She expected Alexa to reprimand her, but her coworker didn't even flinch. "I listened to it over and over. It's not him. There's something odd about the voice recording. Something I can't pinpoint."

"Have Rene listen. She's got a good ear for nailing accents and weird enunciation."

Tika scribbled down a note. "I'll do that. That reporter who confronted Wade could be a suspect, but she seemed more offended at being used than homicidal." Frowning, she looked at Alexa. "Maybe I'm not cut out for this, Lex. I'm missing too much."

And I slept with my client last night, she silently added.

"Maybe I should hand this off to Holly. She probably could have solved this by now."

"Don't let self-doubt start pulling you down. This case is

challenging. Start with the ex," Alexa suggested. "Always start with the ex."

Tika frowned as she flipped to the page of notes she'd made on Erin Diaz. "They broke up because Lisa used a personal conversation between them as a source for a story. Erin got fired over it."

"Ouch," Alexa muttered. "That's a heck of a motive."

"And she had the means. People at the apartment complex knew her and would feel comfortable letting her into the building."

"But?" Alexa asked.

Tika turned her notebook toward her coworker and tapped at the last note. "She was on a date the night Lisa died. Verified alibi. There were photos of them posted on social media around the time that Lisa fell. Erin was too far away to have been in the stairwell at that time."

"Hmm. What about that reporter? The one you said made such a scene?"

"I haven't verified her alibi," Tika said. "But my gut says it wasn't her. She was upset, but not enough to actually confront Lisa, let alone get into a shoving match at the top of a flight of stairs."

Alexa smiled gently. "It might not have been a shoving match, Tik. She might have stepped too close, and Lisa moved back and fell. Even if she *was* confronted, it could have been an accident."

Tika twisted her lips as she looked back at her notes. "If it was an accident, don't you think whoever was with her would have called for help?"

"People rarely react the way you think they should. Especially if they wanted her camera or whatever was on it. Do you have a list of people who had a beef with her?"

Tika snorted as she flipped to another page and presented it like a game show host. "A very long list. I have them broken down as personal reasons, career competition, and targets— meaning people she wrote about or was writing stories about."

Alexa let out a low whistle. "Wow."

"Yeah." Tika frowned as she scanned the list again. "Luckily, I've marked several off. But I feel like..."

"It's a lot," her friend said gently. "But you can do this. I know you can. And we are all here to help."

Tika stared at Dylan Tyler's name before pointing her pen at it. "I interviewed him yesterday. He's hiding something. He didn't do anything off, but I felt it. I could sense he wasn't being honest with me about something. Does that make sense?"

"Yeah. That's your instinct talking. Listen to it. Dig into him more. If you suspect he has secrets, he likely does."

"We all have secrets," Tika muttered, thinking of her night with Wade.

Alexa grinned. "That sounds absolutely intriguing."

"I meant *his* secrets."

"Sure you did," Alexa teased.

Tika tapped her pen again. "Lisa had a file on him. He'd been threatening her because of an old article she'd written that painted him in a very bad light. Apparently, the accusations she'd made had a way of resurfacing when potential employers were doing background searches, and he insisted that was what had cost him more than one job."

Alexa raised her brows. "Oh, yeah. Grab a shovel and

start digging. There's probably a lot more there that you haven't found yet."

"I think I also need to look into other members of the campaign who might have..." Tika's words trailed off when the front door to their office slammed. That never ended well. She glanced at Alexa to verify she'd heard the noise too.

"Did you seriously call my tailor and have my dress altered?" Holly's voice boomed.

"Uh-oh," Tika muttered.

"Shit," Alexa muttered.

"Altered? No," Sam answered. "Added a slit up the side? Yes."

"That's called altering, Sam," Holly stated.

"She's gonna kill her," Alexa said as she and Tika jumped up.

They rushed into the lobby in time to see Holly point her finger at Sam. Tika had never seen so much anger on Holly's face. She tended to be emotionless. Eerily calm. She was not calm now. Not even close.

"You have gone too far," Holly said.

Sam sank back in her chair. "I had a slit added to make dancing easier, Holly."

"It's my wedding dress, Samantha. It's *my* fucking wedding!"

Eva rushed forward from the hallway, where she'd been in her office. "Holly, it's okay. We'll have it fixed."

"Damn straight, and you're paying for it," she informed her receptionist. "And, in case you haven't figured this out, you will no longer make decisions about my wedding."

Tika winced. Sam had been working so hard to make sure

Holly had a beautiful wedding. If it weren't for Sam, Holly would have gone to the courthouse—which Holly said she preferred, but everyone agreed that once the wedding was over, she'd appreciate that Sam put in effort to plan a more personalized wedding.

But Tika had to agree, altering Holly's dress without permission was going too far.

Rene joined the group in the lobby. "What the hell is going on in here?"

Alexa gestured to the standoff. "They're finally having it out over the wedding."

Rolling her eyes, Rene let out a long breath. "For fuck's sake. I thought it was something serious."

"You know what," Sam stated, standing to meet Holly's angry stare as she ignored everyone else, "you can get married in a potato sack on the side of the road for all I care. I am damn tired of your ungratefulness."

"Are you kidding me?" Holly screamed. "I would prefer a potato sack and the side of the road compared to this circus you've been planning. Nothing about this fiasco is what I want for *my* wedding."

"Enough," Rene stated.

However, she might as well have saved her energy. Sam's cheeks flushed, and she narrowed her eyes so much they were barely visible through the long, fake lashes. "You are so rude."

"Stay out of my business," Holly warned.

"Fine," Sam stated and grabbed her purse. "I'm out."

"Wait," Tika called when Sam started for the door.

"Let her go," Holly said and then marched toward her office.

Tika and Alexa looked at each other. "How long do we need to give them to cool down before we try to talk sense into them?"

Alexa shrugged. "An hour or two?"

Nodding, Tika said. "Good. Rene, do you have a few minutes to listen to something with me?"

"Sure," she muttered.

Tika led her to the conference room where she had all the evidence for Lisa's case spread out. "Think they'll work this out?" she asked as she found the file on her laptop.

"Yeah. We all knew it was going to come to this eventually."

Opening the recording, Tika looked at her coworker, hoping she could help her. "This is the voicemail Lisa received a few weeks before her death. I thought it might have been Lawrence Butler or Dylan Tyler, but the voice isn't even close for either of them, and the more I listen to it, the more I think there's something odd about the voice. Something I can't figure out."

"Let's hear it."

Tiki hit play and stood silently as the voice came through her speaker. She played it three times, and each time, Rene tilted her head and her eyes swam as she focused. After the final play-through, she stood upright and relaxed into her usual posture.

"It sounds off because someone used one of those voice apps that can make your voice higher or lower."

Tika closed her eyes. Damn it. Why hadn't she thought of that? Her sense of frustration in herself must have been written on her face, because Rene gave her a supportive smile.

"I only know because Danny found that app on Quinn's phone and won't stop changing his voice. It's making me crazy."

Tika smiled at the mention of the little boy who had won over all of HEARTS when Rene was working his father's case. Quinn and Rene fell for each other while on the job, and Tika very nearly mentioned her night with Wade, but the slamming of an office door drew their attention.

"I swear," Rene whispered, "this wedding can't be over fast enough. I just want things to go back to normal around here." Looking at Tika again, she asked, "Anything else?"

"Um, is there a way to un-filter the filter? I'd like to hear the actual voice if possible."

Rene chuckled. "That I don't know. Eva might have a better idea on that."

"Thanks, Rene." Blowing out her breath, she grabbed her laptop and carried it with her toward Eva's office. However, she stopped when she heard Holly loudly venting behind the closed door. She did not want to interrupt that. The only other person tech savvy enough to know about the filter would be Sam, who had stormed out.

Letting out a long sigh, Tika went back to the conference room, wondering if this was something she could research on the Internet.

WADE WALKED INTO HEARTS AND WAS SURPRISED when the reception desk was empty. Taking the cup holder with two cups of coffee, he glanced around before settling his gaze on the conference room where he'd first met with Tika. Walking that way, he tentatively poked his head in and smiled when he spotted her leaning over the table with papers spread out before her.

"Hey," he said softly. She turned and smiled, and his heart melted. He couldn't even begin to explain the level of disappointment he'd felt when he'd rolled over to find her missing from his bed. It was more than disappointment, it was fear. But seeing her sweet smile eased the concern that she regretted being with him the night before.

Who the hell could regret the way they'd made love? They'd made fireworks.

"Hey," she said in a warm voice.

Lifting the drink carrier, he showed her the excuse he'd made for stopping by unannounced. "I hope it isn't too late for coffee."

She glanced at her watch. "Nope. I appreciate it, actually."

He held out a cup of the mocha drink he'd heard her order several times. "Any luck?"

She bit her lip as if hesitant to share with him. "I knew there was something odd about that voicemail that was left on Lisa's phone, but I couldn't quite figure out what it was."

"And?" he asked as his apprehension instantly grew.

"And it seems that the caller used an app to disguise his voice. I didn't realize how easy it was to do that, but..." She held up her phone and waved it at him. "There are dozens of them. As soon as I played the recording for Rene, she pointed out that the reason the voice sounded odd was because it had been distorted by a filter."

"No," he insisted. "I heard it, it wasn't—"

"Listen," she said. She held her phone to her mouth and recited a childhood rhyme. Then she played it back for him. Her voice sounded almost as deep as his. But as he listened closely, he heard the same odd clip to her voice that they'd heard when listening to the voicemail. That must be an effect of altering the original voice.

His hope seemed to deflate. "Then there's no way to find the caller."

"Not necessarily," Tika said, turning off the annoying playback. "I'm still trying to find a way to undo the filter, or to figure out if that's possible. So far, I'm not having much luck since I don't know which app they used in the first place. I'm still going to do what I can to figure out who made that call. It's just not going to be an ah-ha moment of hearing the right voice. I'm sorry."

"No," he said with a shrug. "It's good to know. To make some progress on that. Any other changes I should know about?"

She nodded and then held up a printout that looked like someone's taxes. He didn't want to know how she'd gotten that. "Dylan Tyler. I had a feeling that he was hiding some-thing. I don't know if this is it, but..."

"What?"

"Eva, one of my coworkers, was able to help me get a hold of Dylan's tax records. This is proof that he was working with Lawrence Butler when Lisa did that interview. I'm wondering if the reason the Butlers had such a negative reaction to Lisa was because of something that Dylan said. Maybe he warned them about speaking to her."

Wade's stomach knotted. "Lawrence Butler keeps coming up, doesn't he?"

Tika nodded. "He does."

"When are you going to question him?"

"Soon," she said, but her voice didn't hold an ounce of conviction. In fact, she sounded completely uncertain.

Wade creased his brow as he eyed her. "Why are you hesitating?"

"Well, for two reasons. The first, because I need more puzzle pieces to fall into place before I figure out what I should be asking him. Everything seems to point back to him. I need to know why."

Wade scoffed. "You should be asking him if he killed my sister."

Tika tilted her chin and cocked a brow at him. "And how do you think he's going to answer that? Do you think he'll break that easily?" She put her hand on his arm and gave him a reassuring smile. "I know you want answers, but if I'm going to get them, I have to have enough evidence to put some pressure on him. You understand that, right?"

He didn't like it, but he understood. She was right. If she walked up to Butler and demanded answers without having something to hold over him, the aspiring congressman would walk away, and Tika would never get another chance to question him again. Even so, it didn't sit well with Wade that they were being passive. He wanted to find out who was responsible for Lisa's death so he could put this stress of not knowing behind him.

"Yeah, I understand," he said. "What's the second reason?"

"He's running for congress. I want to be very certain before I imply he had anything to do with what happened to Lisa. I'm quite certain if we start pointing fingers at him, he's going to hide behind the political privilege he's gaining."

"Doesn't being a politician make him more vulnerable?"

Tika scoffed. "It should, but do you know any politician who is held accountable for what they do?"

"No," he muttered as her phone started to ring.

She turned her back on him and answered. He wasn't listening. His mind was still going over how to approach Lawrence Butler when Tika put her hand on his arm. He lifted a brow when she offered him a slight smile.

"That was a pawn shop just outside of town. They did an intake on a camera that they think could be the one we're looking for."

His heart dropped to his stomach. "Let's go."

He followed her out of the conference room and silently urged her to go faster when she stopped to tell one of her coworkers where she was headed. The woman with long red hair offered to reach out to a detective on Tika's behalf.

Wade did everything he could to rush Tika toward the door, but finally, he lightly put his hand to the small of her back and steered her toward the door. She took the hint and started walking faster. As soon as they stepped outside, she glanced over her shoulder.

"I'm driving," she announced. "You'll get a ticket."

He laughed softly, but she wasn't wrong. If Lisa's camera had been pawned, he wanted to get there, get the camera back into his possession, and find out who the hell had pawned it in the first place. The drive seemed to take forever, but when Tika parked in front of a small brick building, Wade jumped from the car before she even cut the engine.

"Slow down," Tika said.

"I want to get that camera."

"Wade." She took several steps and grabbed his hand. "Hey. We're not getting the camera today."

His racing heart dropped to his stomach. "What?"

"Wade, if Lisa was... If someone hurt her, this could be evidence. It has to be processed properly. Eva called Jack Tarrek, Holly's fiancé. He's a detective. He's going to come and collect the camera so it can be held as potential evidence."

He sank back. "If he takes it, how will we know..."

"Jack... Detective Tarrek will tell us what we need to know." Her reassurance wasn't very reassuring. "Come on."

They walked in, and a man with dark hair turned and smiled at Tika. "Pretty sure our guy used a fake ID when he pawned the camera," he said. He handed over a sheet of paper with the name and license number scratched on it. "See this?" He pointed at a series of numbers. "There should be eight numbers and three letters."

Wade scanned the number and frowned. There was an extra number and a missing letter.

"We got security footage of the sale, though," Jack continued. "Come on."

He led them around the counter to a small back room

where a sweaty short man clicked the mouse of a computer and gestured. "See? Just an hour ago. I called right away."

Jack nodded at the man. "No worries. We know you aren't involved in this."

The man seemed to relax. But then the video started, and he offered Jack a flat smile. "Sorry. Quality isn't so good."

No, it wasn't. Wade squinted, trying to make the pixelated image somehow come together. The man walked into the pawnshop with a cap low on his face and dark sunglasses. He knew he was being recorded. The gray zipped-up sweatshirt was nondescript, as was the plain black baseball cap. Nothing about him was identifiable.

Jack frowned and shook his head. "Does he look at all like anyone on your radar?"

The ounce of hope that had filled Wade faded as he shook his head.

"We can try to pull prints from the camera," Jack offered.

"Wait," Tika said. "Back it up."

The sweaty man did as asked.

"Can you zoom?" she asked.

He pressed a few buttons, and the image grew.

Tika pointed at the screen. "There. When he turns to leave, his jacket bulges. There's an emblem on his shirt."

"I can't make it any bigger," the man said.

She leaned even closer. "You don't have to." She stood upright and eyed Jack. "That's Dylan Tyler. I questioned him earlier about threats he made against Lisa. I felt like he was hiding something. I must have spooked him enough to try to dump evidence."

"Wouldn't he just throw it away?" Wade asked.

Jack snorted. "Not if he thought he could get a few bucks."

"Which he did." The pawnshop owner said. "I get that back, right?"

"You'll get it back," Jack muttered and then looked at Tika. "I'll take it from here."

Wade opened his mouth, but before he could protest, Jack faced him.

"This is a criminal investigation now. I'll speak with Dylan Tyler and determine if there's cause to believe he was involved with what happened to your sister. Do you have anything I need to know going into this?"

"We have emails from Dylan to Lisa with vague threats."

"And a voicemail," Wade offered.

"A voicemail that we haven't been able to trace back to anyone specific," Tika clarified. "The caller used a filter that I haven't been able to counter yet."

"I'll reach out to Sam to get those."

Tika opened her mouth, and Wade and Jack both eyed her. "Uh...Holly and Sam had a bit of a disagreement earlier. Sam isn't there."

Jack pressed the fingers of his right hand to his temple. "Shit. Did Holly fire her?"

Tika shrugged. "It was about fifty-fifty on Holly firing her and Sam quitting. I'm sure they'll work it out."

Jack blew out a big breath. "I hope. Sam has been the topic of Holly's ire for the last few weeks. I'm surprised she hasn't dragged me to the courthouse to get the wedding done and put an end to Sam's interference." With a shake of his head, he seemed to try to dislodge the thought and refocus.

"All right. Have *someone* send me the files you have, and I'll work on getting Dylan Tyler in to explain to me all about that camera."

Though Wade was initially disappointed that Tika wouldn't be pressing Dylan Tyler for answers, he was relieved the police were finally taking his concerns seriously. Tika turned and smiled at him, and he realized he was also relieved that some of the issues standing between them would be resolved once the police took over Lisa's case.

[10]

Tika knocked on Sam's door but didn't wait for Sam to answer before pushing it open. As soon as she stepped into the apartment, ignoring the shoes that seemed to have been carelessly tossed aside and the small box of Sam's belongings from HEARTS, Tika chuckled. The chalkboard facing the doorway where Sam liked to leave reminders to herself had chalk in big, bold letters that read, *Go away!*

Instead of heeding the advice, Tika called out to her friend, "Hey, I brought pizza."

"I'm not hungry," Sam yelled from the other room.

Tika followed her voice and found Sam sitting on the big gray sofa with an open soda can, an empty bag of chips, and a candy bar wrapper on the rustic farmhouse-style table in front of her.

Sam's apartment had the trendiest decor, but Tika never thought the place looked like Sam belonged there. She thought Sam belonged in some fancy downtown loft with furniture too expensive to sit on with some poor, smitten man falling at her feet.

Something about Sam always made Tika think she would end up with that kind of lifestyle someday. Maybe it was her fascination with Hollywood stars and movie gossip or her perfectly primped appearance. *Usually* perfectly primped. At the moment, she was a mess. Even with her hair pulled up in a ponytail and her work clothes replaced with pajamas, Sam looked too upper class for the farm style she had used on her apartment.

Tika gestured toward the empty food packages on the table. "I'd guess not after all that. Stuffing your emotions down with junk food?"

"I meant to stop and get groceries on the way home, but I was too mad. I probably would have shoved a mango up someone's ass."

"That's a pleasant image," Tika muttered. "Lucky for you, I am here to save the day." She sat next to Sam and pushed the trash aside to make room for the pizza box.

"I don't want to talk about Holly. I hate her," Sam said from behind the tissue she used to wipe her nose.

"No, you don't." She flipped the top back. "Pepperoni and jalapeño. Your favorite."

Sam sat forward and examined the pizza before taking the slice with the most peppers. "Is this to celebrate solving your first case?"

"I didn't solve anything. Dylan was dumb enough to pawn evidence."

"You identified him," Sam offered. "That means you

solved it." As she grabbed a slice of pizza, she said, "I love you. But I do hate her."

"If you hated her, you wouldn't be so upset."

After stuffing half a slice into her mouth, Sam shook her head. "Not true. I'm upset because even though I hate Holly, I loved my job."

"Sam," Tika pleaded as she pulled a jalapeño off her pizza, "you can't quit."

"I was fired."

"No, you weren't."

Sam took another big bite before saying, "She told me to leave."

"She didn't mean it. You know she didn't mean it."

"Well, I mean it." Sam nodded as if to confirm what she'd decided. She took a big drink from her can of soda and held it up. "There's more in the fridge if you want one."

Tika shook her head. "Don't change the subject."

"I'm not going to put up with Holly's nasty moods anymore."

"She had a point," Tika insisted. "You can't just make changes to someone's wedding dress without talking to her first."

"I didn't have it dyed neon green. I added a slit so that she could move more easily."

"But that's a decision for her to make."

Sam's lip quivered, but she rolled her shoulders back and jutted her chin out. That move was usually saved for when she was digging her heels in to do battle with their boss. "She told me to make things as easy as possible for her. That's what I was doing."

"Sam," Tika said gently, "you've been pushing the boundaries on this wedding for a long time."

"If left up to Holly, her wedding would be a boring disaster."

"By whose standards?" Tika asked gently.

Sam sank back slightly. "If she didn't want me to help, she should have said so."

"Honey, she did," Tika said.

Sam didn't argue. "She let me do this because she was afraid she'd plan a bad wedding and disappoint Jack and his mom."

"Yeah."

"I might have gotten carried away, but that doesn't justify her reaction over a slit in her dress."

"I don't think it was the slit. I think it was everything coming to a head. Yes, you are right, she would likely regret it if she didn't do something nicer than eloping at the courthouse, but you still have to remember Holly is very simplistic. She isn't interested in all the fancy things that you are. You've been inserting too much of yourself into her wedding."

"Well," Sam stated with a slight pout, "she won't have to worry about that anymore. Look, I don't want to talk about Holly."

"Good, let's talk about this case."

"The one you just solved?"

Tika scoffed. She appreciated Sam's enthusiasm but wasn't buying into it. "Until Dylan confesses or Jack can pin her death on him, there's something else that has been bothering me. The voicemail that Lisa received had a weird sound to it. I had Rene listen, and she said she thinks it's a filter."

"He disguised his voice *and* failed to identify himself? How was Lisa supposed to fix whatever she'd done if she didn't know who was calling?"

Tika shrugged and picked another hot pepper off her slice. "Maybe the caller didn't realize that she screwed over every person she ever met."

"Fair assumption," Sam muttered.

"Do you know how I can remove the filter?"

"Not unless you know what filter the caller used."

Tika let out a long sigh. "I don't. Damn it, Sam. I'm hitting another brick wall."

"Calm down," Sam said. "You can use another filter to adjust the pitch and see if you recognize the voice as belonging to someone you've been talking to. Now, that is definitely not something that would be considered hard evidence, but it might give you another lead if Dylan isn't the bad guy."

Another heavy breath left Tika as the weight of everything seemed to crash down on her. She had been so confident when she'd sat Holly down and made a case for why she was ready to be an investigator. Like the true nerd that she was, Tika had spent hours finding evidence to back up her claim and prove herself. But here she was, in the thick of her first case, and she couldn't make sense of anything.

Not to mention that she'd slept with her very first client.

Man, this entire thing was a disaster. She was a disaster. And she was *so* disappointed in herself.

Sam tilted her head. "What's the matter? Why are you beating yourself up when you should be celebrating?"

"This is so much harder than I thought it would be," she

confessed. "Everyone else makes it look so easy. Holly and Rene can solve cases in their sleep. Eva and Alexa can sniff out lies like hound dogs and I..." Frowning as tears bit at the back of her eyes, Tika said, "Sam, I don't know if I'm cut out for this."

Sam gawked at Tika as if she'd said the most ridiculous thing. Grabbing Tika's hand, Sam smiled softly. "What are you talking about? Dylan is getting questioned about Lisa's death right now."

"Because he pawned her camera, not because I made some huge breakthrough."

Lifting her brow, Sam asked, "How did they know it was Dylan?"

"I recognized the emblem on his shirt, but—"

"*You* recognized the emblem. *You* took fliers to all the pawnshops with the serial number to Lisa's camera. *You* put the pieces together."

Tika didn't want to pout, but she couldn't stop her shoulders from sagging and her lip from sticking out a bit. "I got lucky. The others don't get lucky. They figure things out. Maybe I should stick to answering legal questions."

"Don't you do that," Sam stated firmly. "Don't you dare start doubting yourself. You've worked so hard to get your first case. Do not start letting it get to you. This is new and scary, but you can do this, Tik. You can do this. As much as I hate Holly right now—and I *do*—she won't let you fail. If you're feeling this unsure, talk to her about it. She won't think less of you if you need help."

"I know," Tika muttered. "I really wanted to prove myself."

"You are proving yourself," Sam insisted. "Tik, this isn't like you. What's going on here?"

Tika bit her lip, not wanting to confess, but then the words she'd been fighting all day tumbled out of her. "I slept with him."

Sam inhaled dramatically and opened her eyes wider than Tika had ever seen them. "You did *what?*"

Tika scrunched up her nose and nodded. "I know it was wrong."

"Oh, *please*," Sam said with a chuckle. "We might as well add matchmaking to our list of services with the way you guys are always hooking up with the men who walk into that office."

"I didn't mean to," Tika said. "I tried to wait. He's just so...adorable. I couldn't resist him."

"Likely story."

"Thanks for not judging me."

Sam shrugged. "Who am I to judge anything? I can't even land a guy that Holly doesn't run off. Then again"—she picked a pepper off her pizza and popped it into her mouth—"I guess I don't have to worry about that anymore."

Tika debated if she should point out the truth before jumping in. "She runs them off because you have terrible taste in men, Samantha."

"I know," she admitted. Then she grinned. "But the bad ones are oh-so good."

Sadness filled Tika's chest as she and Sam shared a light laugh. "I'm going to miss working with you. Are you sure you don't want to try to work things out with Holly?"

"I'm positive. You can come see me anytime. You know where I am."

"Yes, I do," Tika said and leaned over to pull her phone from her pocket when it rang. "It's Jack. Hey," she said as a way of greeting the detective who had gone out of his way to help the HEARTS since he started dating their fearless leader. Jack and Holly were a matched pair if Tika had ever seen one, but she also knew he didn't have to go out of his way to keep the team in the loop once the police got involved with their cases.

"Dylan Tyler wants to make a deal," Jack said.

"What kind of deal?" Tika asked.

"He says Lawrence Butler was having an affair and Lisa had the proof. You know anything about that?"

"I know that Lisa thought there was more to the Butler's marriage than they were letting on. There were a lot of photos in Lisa's research that wouldn't be flattering if made public, but most of those were from Butler's younger years. I didn't see anything that would imply he was having an affair, but Lisa thought the Butlers were hiding something. It could have been adultery, but as far as I know, she didn't have any evidence."

"He says the proof is on the SD card he took from Lisa's camera."

Tika sat a bit taller. The camera that Wade had insisted had been stolen from his sister. "Did Dylan happen to say how he got that camera?"

Jack hesitated.

Tika waited several heartbeats before whispering, "My God. Did he push Lisa down the stairs?"

"No. He has an alibi."

Again, she waited, but he didn't explain. "What? What's his alibi?"

"He was at a bar drinking away his sorrows until he left at around nine o'clock. There's security footage. He's covered."

Tika was quiet for a moment. "The ambulance was called for Lisa at just after nine fifteen. How far was this bar from Lisa's apartment?"

"Too far for him to be involved."

"Damn," she whispered. "He got that camera somehow, Jack."

"Apparently, Lisa found out Lawrence Butler was having an affair. She followed him around until she got pictures to prove it. But she wasn't as sneaky as she thought. Dylan Tyler spotted her slinking around the hotel where he works. He confronted her, she told him to get over it, and left. He says that was the last time he saw her, but he did tell someone on the Butler campaign that he had seen someone taking pictures of the candidate. He said he'd tell Lawrence Butler in exchange for a job on the campaign. I guess he had political ambitions."

"Yeah," Tika said, "he had to rethink his goals after Lisa implied he engaged in racist activities a few years ago."

"So," Jack said, "he was more than happy to give Lisa's name to Lawrence Butler."

"But he wasn't working for the campaign. When I interviewed him, he was still doing security at the hotel."

"Tyler says they were working on making room for him."

"All the clues keep going back to Lawrence Butler," Tika said quietly. "He is right in the middle of this."

"I doubt that's a coincidence," Jack said.

"Same. So Lisa got photos of him cheating on his wife the night she died in a fall that may or may not have been an accident." She scoffed. "Something is definitely off there, Jack."

"I agree. I'm going to need you to get me all the information you have on this, Tika. It's out of your hands now."

"Got it," she said and frowned. She had known he'd likely take over the case, but she'd had to call him anyway. Jack was good to the women of HEARTS, but he did have his limits. Murder evidence? Not something he was going to let the PIs handle. "I'll head to the office now. I can email most of it."

"Thanks, Tika."

Heaving a sigh, she looked at Sam. "He's taking my case."

"So he's starting to suspect Lisa might have been murdered?"

"Well, at the very least, there's now proof that someone stole her camera." Pushing herself up, she wiped her hands on a napkin and then tossed it onto the coffee table. "Call Holly. Apologize."

"No."

"Sam," she stated. "Just do it so we can all get back to normal."

"Who the hell wants that?" Sam asked. "I'm not apologizing, Tik. I'm tired of how she treats me. I'm not the burden she makes me out to be."

"Nobody said you're a burden."

"She treats me like one. And I'm done with it."

Tika frowned instead of pointing out that Sam could try harder, she could take her job more seriously, and she could definitely learn some boundaries. Now wasn't the time to delve into that.

"So what are you going to do?"

Sam grabbed a slice of pizza. "Eat my dinner and watch a movie. We'll chat tomorrow."

Rather than continue to debate, Tika left Sam to mope. She called Wade as she headed toward her car. He deserved an update on what was happening with Lisa's case. He deserved to know that he was right—someone had taken Lisa's camera, which meant there really could be something suspicious about his sister's death.

As soon as Wade hung up the phone, rage filled him. He had been telling Tika for weeks that Lawrence Butler had something to do with Lisa's death. He'd known it. As soon as he found out Lisa was questioning the politician, Wade had known in his gut that the sleazy man with the forced smile had something to do with her death.

Tika insisted the evidence was pointing to this Dylan Tyler person, but she also said that the photos were tied back to Butler. That was all the confirmation that Wade needed. Opening his laptop, he brought up the website he had been obsessing over for weeks. The campaign site for Lawrence Butler had a list of events for the politician.

Wade checked his watch and then grabbed his keys and headed for the hotel where the man was scheduled to speak. He found it interesting that this was the third event at the same hotel where Dylan Tyler worked.

If that didn't scream conspiracy, he didn't know what did.

Clearly they were working together to cover up what Butler had done. Wade didn't know why. Maybe Dylan was trying to prove his loyalty to get a spot on Butler's security team or a role on the campaign. Or his motives could have been as old as time—money.

Whatever the reason, those two were tied together, and now Tyler was tied to Lisa's camera.

He sped his way to the hotel and parked in the public lot across the street. Then he rushed through the lobby of the old building. Instead of waiting for the elevator, Wade took the ornate staircase to the second floor. The decor reminded him of his grandmother's house—everything was too pretty and fragile to serve an actual purpose, and nobody was allowed to touch anything.

However, once he neared the ballroom, the decor changed to something much more modern. Balloons floated, and flashy signs encouraged people to volunteer and vote for Lawrence Butler.

A woman with a dozen or so buttons attached to a ribbon across her chest was encouraging people to take stickers, posters, and yard signs. When he noticed a man in a suit with an earpiece in, Wade focused on the table, as if looking over the free offerings, while the woman got contact information from someone willing to volunteer for the campaign.

"Sir?" the man asked with a deep voice that, for some reason, reminded Wade of a bear growling out a warning.

Wade cringed inside but glanced up and smiled, relieved when he was met with a curious gaze instead of claws and fangs. "Good evening."

"Can I help you?"

"I'm here for the event."

The man who seemed to be security looked over Wade's wrinkled button-down shirt and slacks. "Do you have a ticket?"

"Uh. Press," Wade blurted out. "I'm a member of the press."

Again, the man looked him over, clearly not buying his story. "Where's your media pass?"

Wade patted himself and looked down. "Oh shoot. I must have lost it somewhere."

The man leaned his head back and peered at Wade. "Come back when you find it."

"Yeah," Wade said. "Okay." He turned and headed back the way that he'd arrived but made a show of stopping to peer at things. Finally, the guard turned around to speak to someone else. He glanced back at Wade one more time before moving farther down the hallway to deal with something or someone else.

Wade pulled out his phone and pretended to text someone, but as soon as the guard was far enough away, Wade slipped into the ballroom. A few people glanced at him, and he realized that he was never going to blend in. He'd spent the day in the classroom. His clothes were wrinkled, while every other man in the room wore crisp suits. The women were dressed in suits as well, some with slacks, some with skirts, and others wore dresses. Even the waitstaff had on nicer clothes than Wade.

Oh well. He wasn't here to make friends. He was here to call out Lawrence Butler for what he'd done to Lisa.

"Sir," someone called as Wade scanned the crowd for the distinguished Mr. Butler.

Wade glanced back to confirm that a woman in a suit with a clipboard was in fact speaking to him. Rather than acknowledge her, he moved farther into the room.

"Sir," she called more loudly. "I need to see your ticket."

Wade didn't stop. There, across the room, Lawrence Butler beamed as he smiled for a photo with an elderly couple. The man looked absolutely smug. Exactly the way Wade pictured he'd be. Full of himself, not a care in the world, and not an ounce of remorse for hurting innocent people to climb his way to the top.

The anger in Wade's belly ignited and propelled him forward. He was nearing the man when a petite woman stepped in front of him and pressed her hands to his chest to stop him in his tracks. He immediately recognized her from the photos Lisa had taken. Karen Butler.

She plastered an obviously fake smile to her red-painted lips. "I do believe Kari was asking for your ticket." She hesitated, as if waiting for him to present what she'd requested, but then her smile softened to faux sympathy. He immediately realized why Lisa didn't buy her act. This woman was as fake as anyone he'd ever seen. "I'm so sorry, but this is a paid event for supporters only. If you'd like to—"

"I'm Lisa Steele's brother," he stated, and as he expected, Karen's eyes flickered with panic for a moment before her defenses slid into place.

"Well, I'm sorry for your loss."

"Are you?" he asked.

She leaned back and arched a dark brow at him. "Of course."

"Is your husband?"

The panic flashed again before she gestured for someone to join her. The same security guard who'd stopped Wade from entering the first time appeared at her side.

"Please show Mr. Steele to the door. And make sure he uses it."

"Yes, ma'am," the guard said.

"Hey," Wade yelled toward the politician, not willing to give up that easily.

Lawrence glanced his way but quickly returned his attention to the woman trying to take a selfie with him. The smile he had on his face was the same fake, forced smile that Wade suspected was the reason Lisa wanted to dig into the politician.

"Sir," the guard warned.

Wade ignored him, "I want to talk to you! About what you did to my sister!"

"Wade," Tika said, grabbing his other arm. She widened her eyes and shook her head in a silent warning to stop while he was ahead.

He hadn't told her where he was headed, but he figured he shouldn't be surprised that she'd figured it out. She'd said she was on her way to his place. When he wasn't there, she probably hadn't had to think too much about where he'd gone.

"He killed my sister," Wade said, surprised at how his voice cracked. All these weeks of trying to prove what he knew had taken more of a toll on him than he'd realized. He'd been so focused on getting answers that he hadn't really let himself feel the impact of what he'd been trying to prove.

Someone—Lawrence Butler, it seemed—had taken his sister from him. Lisa had been taken from him, leaving a void that would never be filled. Leaving an ache that would never be soothed. His sister was gone. Forever. And that man with his cocky grin was responsible.

"He killed her," Wade said again, with more conviction.

Several people gasped, and murmurs filled his ears. As he looked around the gathering, he stopped when he met a pair of familiar eyes. Sheryl Hunter had a tape recorder in her hand, aimed in Wade's direction. There was an odd look on her face. She seemed...excited. There was an underlying hunger in her eyes that he'd seen before. On his sister.

Whenever Lisa got an idea for a story or a tip that she thought was going to boost her career, she'd get that same glimmer in her eyes. He'd admired it on her, but on Sheryl the look was eerie. Cold. Perhaps it had been cold on Lisa too, and Wade hadn't seen it that way. But he knew it. He knew that look.

Sheryl Hunter had caught the scent of her next big story.

Wade might have been offended any other time, but right now, seeing as she was the only one who seemed interested in the truth, he opened his mouth, ready to tell her all about it.

"That's enough," the guard said. His voice made it clear he wasn't kidding.

"Hush," Tika warned under her breath when Wade started to speak despite the warning.

He ignored her warning. This was the only chance he was probably going to get to confront this man.

Looking over Karen's head, Wade returned his attention to Lawrence. However, his arm was twisted painfully behind his back before he could scream the angry words that he'd been holding on to since he'd come to realize that man was responsible for Lisa's death. A hand pressed to his spine, causing him to cry out as he was led from the room.

"Please," Tika begged whoever had Wade twisted in the awkward position, "let him go. I'll make sure he leaves."

The guard walked them to the elevator and roughly punched the button before easing his hold on Wade. "If I see him again, I'm calling the police."

"You won't see him again," Tika said.

Tika held Wade when he turned back toward the ballroom. He wasn't going anywhere. He knew he'd never get back in there now. As he stared, Karen Butler stepped out into the hallway. She caught his gaze and held it. Something in her eyes was unsettling, even from a distance. Once again, Wade realized why his sister found this woman so off-putting. There was something about Karen, something that didn't seem right.

"Enough," Tika whispered when she caught Wade staring at the woman. "You're going to get yourself in real trouble, Wade." Tika tugged at his arm until he broke the staring contest with Karen. He looked at the woman next to him, and she shook her head. "You cannot just barge into events and start accusing people of murder. What's wrong with you?"

Despite his irritation, he let her guide him into the elevator. She practically punched a button before facing him. "What the hell were you thinking?"

"He—"

"The police are involved in this now, Wade," she stated. "This is no longer you and me looking for clues. They have evidence that they have to follow up on. The right way. If Lawrence Butler had anything to do with what happened to Lisa—"

"If?"

"*If,*" she stated again. "You just tipped him off. You fool."

The elevator doors opened, and Tika marched out, clearly furious at Wade. As soon as he realized the point she was making, he didn't blame her. He'd made a huge mistake. "I'm sorry."

"You should be." She rolled her eyes and relaxed. "Wade, I know this is hard on you, but you have to let the people who know what they're doing take over. You did your part. You pushed and pushed until someone listened. That's all you can do. It's out of your hands now. It's out of *our* hands."

He nodded before giving her a pathetic smile. "Forgive me?"

"Don't try to win me over with puppy dog eyes, Wade. You could have been arrested," she said through clenched teeth. "You could have tipped him off and sent him running."

"I know. I'm sorry."

"Sorry? Wade! This could have just turned into the murder investigation that you've been pushing for, and you almost blew it before it started."

"I said I'm sorry," he said, almost as angrily. "That was my sister, Tika. He hurt her..."

"Wade," Tika said more gently, "until the police finish their investigation, it's *if—if he hurt her.* You can't go running around throwing out accusations, especially toward a politician in a very public setting."

"I get it."

"Do you?"

Closing the distance between them, he put his hand on her face. "Yes. I'm sorry, Tika. I just lost my head."

Her anger softened under his touch. "I know. I get it. I know this is a lot for you."

Leaning down, he kissed her softly. "I'm glad you're here," he whispered.

Putting her hands on his hips, she pulled him closer. "Me too."

After sharing a long, deep kiss, Wade leaned back. "Do you think it was Butler who pushed her?" he asked. "Or did Dylan Tyler do the dirty work?"

She rolled her eyes but then shook her head and muttered, "Politicians never do their own dirty work. If it wasn't Dylan, it was someone else on Butler's payroll."

"This Jack person... He'll figure that out, right?"

Tika nodded. "Yeah. Jack will figure it out." Reaching out, she put her hand on his. "You've done all you can, Wade. Let the police take it from here."

Rather than lying by telling her he would, he stepped toward the door as it slid open. He started to reach into his pocket to dig his keys out, but Tika grabbed his arm and shook her head.

"Oh no, big boy. You're coming with me."

Wade was about to protest, but she pulled him in the opposite direction of where he'd parked his car.

Tika made Wade ride back to his house with her. She didn't trust him to go home without rushing back into the hotel and getting himself arrested. She didn't speak to him all the way back to his little one-story home, though. She was far too angry. While she understood where he was coming from, she didn't understand why he would rush off and confront Lawrence Butler like that.

Tipping off a suspect was definitely not on the list of ways to solve a case. Yes, his emotions had gotten the better of him, but damn it, why couldn't he just trust her and Jack to handle this?

"I need—" He started as she turned onto his block.

"Nope," she stated, cutting him off. "Do not speak to me yet. I'm not calm enough to deal with this."

Wade sank back in his seat and crossed his arms. He sat that way, like a pouty child, until she turned into his driveway. Once she cut the ignition, she looked at him. "You could have blown any chance we had at nailing Lawrence Butler."

"How so?"

Cocking a brow at him, she took a deep breath. "Let's say he had evidence somewhere of what happened to Lisa. Now that he knows you know, do you think he's going to keep that evidence around? Or do you think he's going to double back and make sure every track he could have possibly left is erased?"

Wade frowned again. "He killed her."

"If he did, we need to let the police handle it. Jack is on this now, Wade."

He looked at her in the dim light that filled the car. "I needed to confront him."

"Well. Maybe you should have waited."

Releasing her seatbelt, she climbed from the car and waited at the bumper for him to join her.

"Are you going to be babysitting me now?" he asked with a clip.

Tika stared at him. "Do you need a babysitter? I can call one of my coworkers. They'd be glad to keep your ass at home. Or I can come in and keep you company."

Relaxing, he rolled his head from side to side before looking at her again. "I'm sorry. I guess I'm a little testy."

"You think?"

A slight smile curved his lips in that way that made him look like a sad sap seeking understanding. "I think my blood sugar is a little low."

"Then I think you need to eat."

He didn't make a move toward the house. Instead, he hesitantly took her hand. "I am sorry. I let my anger get the better of me. I see now how stupid that was. I hope I didn't make things harder for you and Detective Tarrek."

"I'm sure we'll work it out. Come on. You need food before I have to put you in an arm lock like that guard did."

"You laugh," he said as he turned toward the house, "but that hurt."

"I have no doubt," she said as they started up the stairs to the front door. As he unlocked the house, she told him all about her training and how Holly and Rene used to twist her arm just like that to show her how easy it could be for someone to get the upper hand on her if she weren't paying attention.

"This is what you guys do for fun?" Wade asked.

"Not Sam and me. The others? Yeah, because they are demented."

They shared a soft laugh before Wade tossed his keys on the coffee table and shoved his hands in his pockets. "I need you to do something for me."

"Oh, boy," she moaned.

"I need to listen to that voicemail again."

"Wade," Tika said through gritted teeth.

Putting his hands on her face, he waited for her to look at him. "He did this, Tika. I know he did. Help me prove it."

Tika withheld the urge to scream at him to stop fixating on Lawrence Butler and to let Jack and his department take over the investigation. She'd done what he'd hired her to do. She'd gotten enough evidence to get the police involved. Now he needed to back off and let them do their job. But when she stopped being so frustrated with his determination to pin this on the politician that Lisa had been laser focused on, Tika understood where he was coming from.

If anything like this ever happened to one of her siblings, she wouldn't stop either. In fact, she'd probably be far more unhinged than Wade. All in all, he was handling himself incredibly well, and she needed to give him credit for that.

"Can we just try?" Wade asked. "Please."

Tika nodded. "I need to get my laptop out of the car. If you sneak out…"

He smirked at her. "I won't." Holding up three fingers he said, "Science teacher's honor."

She giggled. "For whatever that's worth."

Grabbing her hand, he pulled her to him. "It's worth a lot. Trust me." After giving her a soft kiss, he whispered. "I just need to know if that was him calling her."

"Okay," Tika said. "I'll be right back." She dug her keys from her purse and rushed out to her car. The lights flashed and a quick honk sounded as she used her remote to unlock the doors. As she closed in on her vehicle, she popped the trunk and grabbed her laptop bag. After putting the strap over her shoulder, she slammed the trunk and locked the car. She turned back toward the house and paused when she noticed the front door open. She thought she'd closed it but must not have in her rush to get outside.

"Were you born in a barn?" Tika muttered to herself as she considered what her mother would say. She eased the door closed behind her. "All right," she said as she headed into the living room, "we are giving this fifteen minutes…" Her voice trailed off as she eased the bag off her shoulder and looked around the room. "Wade?"

Where had he gone?

"If he sneaked out when I wasn't looking," she said under her breath. "Wade!"

"I'm in the kitchen," he called from the other room.

When she walked in, she laughed lightly at herself. Of course he was in the kitchen. Had they not just had an entire conversation about how he needed sustenance before he turned into a bear? For a moment, she really had thought that he'd slipped out to confront Lawrence Butler again. Instead, he was in the kitchen putting a bag of popcorn into the microwave. He hit the button to start the microwave and stepped around the island where she'd set her laptop.

She grinned when he wrapped his arms around her waist and kissed her neck. "You're damn lucky you were in the kitchen and not running out on me," she told him.

He smiled. "I'll never run out on you. Listen, about earlier... I'm sorry. I want you to know that I hear what you're saying. I lost my cool, and that could have blown the investigation. I'll reign it in going forward."

"That's a big promise."

"One I intend to keep. If we are able to identify the voice on the recording, I'll sit right next to you while you reach out to Jack. Okay?"

"Okay," she said. She kissed him lightly before moving to the island. Within a few minutes, her laptop was up and running, and she opened the app Sam had suggested for altering the pitch on the recording.

She glanced at him once the recording was loaded and ready to play with. "This isn't proof of anything, Wade. It's information—hopefully good information to lead us in the right direction—but it *isn't* proof."

"I know," he said softly.

With that, she pressed play, and the familiar voice filled the room. As soon as Tika lowered the pitch, she knew that was the wrong direction. If anyone had a voice that deep, they would certainly have remembered it. Instead, she pushed the digital bar higher, higher, and higher until she creased her brow and looked at the man next to her.

"Wait..." Her voice trailed as she listened. Finally, a light bulb went off in her mind. "Have we been completely wrong about this?"

The crease between Wade's brows deepened, and he shook his head slightly. Slowly, he seemed to come to the same conclusion that she had. "It's a woman," he said. "Go higher."

Tika eased the bar up and played the recording again. "Definitely a woman."

Wade scoffed. "Sheryl Hunter."

Tika listened again. Closer. "I don't think so."

"Did you see the light in her eyes when she heard me say Butler killed Lisa? I thought she was ready to pounce to get the story, but maybe she saw her chance to pin it on someone else."

"Her voice is...different. Mousier than this one. This voice is...husky." Again, Tika altered the pitch and played it back. She listened closer and closed her eyes so she could focus. Turning her face to him, she jerked her eyes open. "Oh my God," Tika said, standing back and looking at Wade with wide eyes. "That's Karen Butler."

Wade shook his head. "No. It can't be."

Tika opened a new window on her computer. Within moments, she found an interview with the Butlers. She fast-forwarded through the footage until Karen Butler's smiling face appeared. Hitting play, she turned up the volume, and they listened intently. Then Tika played the voicemail from Lisa's file, adjusted the voice again, and hit play.

Standing upright, Tika eyed Wade. "That is definitely Karen Butler."

The color had faded from Wade's face. He could no longer deny what was obvious. Instead of insisting she was wrong, he scoffed. "Karen Butler left that voicemail threatening Lisa."

"That doesn't prove anything, Wade," Tika was quick to point out. "We already knew she had all but told Lisa she wouldn't get close to Lawrence again. Leaving her a voicemail doesn't prove that Karen had anything to do with Lisa's death."

Wade's cheeks paled further at the mention of his sister. "Maybe not yet, but something tells me it could. We need to call Detective Tarrek and let him know."

"Actually," Karen stated as she walked into the room, "I'd rather you didn't."

From where Tika and Wade stood, facing her on the other side of the island, Karen looked as calm and collected as she ever had. The prim, petite woman was still wearing the black suit from earlier in the evening with the Vote Butler button on the lapel. Her hair was still in the neat updo that made her look like the perfect political wife.

She was the same put-together woman from the event

earlier in the evening. The only difference now was the handgun she had aimed in their direction.

Wade started to move to put himself between Tika and Karen, but Tika held her hand out to him and stood her ground. She glanced at him and gave a slight shake of her head. Until she knew how serious Karen was about shooting them, they needed to stay still and stay calm. Surprising someone with a gun was never a good idea.

Lifting her hands, Tika eased her tense posture and said, "Karen, put the gun down before someone gets hurt."

Karen smiled in an eerily sweet way—she was far too aware for Tika to consider her to be unstable. Which meant she was simply evil, and that was far more terrifying to her. Evil was much more difficult to maneuver.

"Really?" Karen asked with the same tone someone might order coffee. "I'm aiming a loaded gun at you, and you think I'm worried about someone getting hurt?" Rolling her eyes, she shook her head. "It was an accident," she stated. "A stupid accident. I just needed her to hand over the camera, and she wouldn't do it."

"What?" Wade asked with a quivering voice.

Tika wanted to hush him, but she was too shocked to respond. Did Karen just admit to killing Lisa? *Karen?*

"I..." Karen stuttered for a moment in the first show of a crack in her exterior. "I didn't mean for her to fall." Her eyes were glassy for a moment, but she blinked several times and cleared her throat, as if silently reminding herself to keep it together.

Wade swayed next to Tika. She didn't blame him. This woman had just admitted to killing his sister. But there was nothing Tika could do to soothe him. Not right now. Not when the woman was holding a gun on them.

"I just needed the camera," Karen said again with a sad tone as if she were disappointed over the weather instead of admitting to having a part in someone's death, "but she wouldn't hand it over. I didn't mean for her to fall. You under-stand that, right?"

"But she did fall," Tika said calmly as she slowly moved to the right, closer to being able to round the island.

Karen's eyes swam as if she were reliving the moment Lisa died. "She slipped and...she let out this little yelp as she fell. I told her not to run with that story about Lawrence. She didn't listen. She wouldn't listen. And then...she took pictures." Blinking, Karen looked at Wade. "I didn't mean for her to die."

Wade softly asked, "Did she suffer?"

"No," Karen said and gave him an eerily sympathetic smile. "She was dead when she hit the bottom."

Tika slipped her hand into his. That was as much support as she could offer when a madwoman was holding a gun on them.

"Okay," Tika said soothingly. "Lisa's death was an acci-dent. But what you're doing now, Karen, this is not acciden-tal. You're holding a gun on us."

She turned her focus to Wade. "You shouldn't have said what you did about Lawrence." Her brow creased as if she were disappointed in a child. "And you said it in front of all those people. And that reporter."

Tika smiled. "Nobody believed him."

"She did," Karen insisted. "And now...well, her blood is on your hands, isn't it?"

Tika's heart flipped in her chest, but rather than asking for clarification, she continued using a soft, calming tone. "Your supporters won't listen to gossip like that. They know Lawrence couldn't hurt anyone."

Karen smirked at her. "Don't try to placate me. I know better than anyone what my husband is capable of. I've spent most of our marriage cleaning up his messes. I didn't do all that to see his career end now. He's going to Washington," she stated. "He could be president someday. But not with accusations of murder being tossed about."

Tika's breath hitched when Karen raised the gun again. "We don't have any evidence."

Tilting her head, Karen sighed. "I just confessed to being there when that bitch fell. I know Dylan is being questioned. He'll keep his mouth shut if he knows what's good for him, but you... You've already opened yours, and now I need to shut it."

She lifted the gun, taking aim at Wade. Without thinking, Tika lurched around the corner of the island and headed right for Karen. The woman pulled the trigger, and a shot rang out.

Tika's heart nearly stopped, but her feet didn't. She gripped Karen's wrist and twisted it much the way the security guard had done to Wade earlier, and then punched Karen in the side of the face.

By the time Wade reached them, Tika had Karen face down on the tile floor with her arms bent behind her back. Her pearl necklace had snapped, and little beads rolled around her as she screamed out in pain.

"Gun," Tika said. "Wade!"

"Huh?" he asked, blinking a few times.

"Kick the gun away so she can't get it!"

"Right." He used his toes to push the gun away. "Now what?"

Tika looked up at him. "Are you hit?"

"No."

"Okay," she said with relief. "Call 9-1-1 and tell them we need the police."

At that, Karen jerked under Tika and started screaming incoherently. Tika grunted as she pressed her knee into Karen's back and tugged her arm harder.

"Don't move," Tika warned.

"You're hurting me!"

"Good." Tika looked up and blew a strand of hair from her eyes. "Wade. Call for help, please."

He finally snapped out of the daze he was in and fumbled to pull his phone from his pocket. As he dialed 9-1-1, Tika looked at the woman beneath her.

"Something tells me your husband's career is about to tank, and it had nothing to do with Lisa, Wade, or Sheryl. I think he can thank you wholeheartedly for that."

Karen grunted as she relaxed under Tika's hold.

Wade sat on the front steps of his house, watching the activity. Police officers came and went, occasionally stopping to ask him a question or two. Tika stood in the yard talking to Jack Tarrek and Holly Austin. As soon as the police had arrived and taken over the scene, Tika had told them that Karen had implied that she'd killed Sheryl Hunter.

Karen had been arrested, and the police had set up a perimeter to keep all the onlookers at bay. While all this was happening, Wade stared at his phone and tried to work up the courage to call his parents. The police wouldn't let him leave, and he didn't want them to hear on the news that a politician's wife had tried to shoot him. However, he was still trying to process the entire situation himself. He couldn't quite grasp what was happening.

When Jack arrived on the scene with Holly, he told Tika and Wade that the police had found Sheryl's body outside the hotel. Apparently she'd left soon after Wade had been escorted out of the event. Karen must have followed her and made certain she didn't start digging into Wade's accusation.

Logically, Wade knew it was Karen, and Karen alone, who was responsible for killing Sheryl, but he still felt guilt creeping up on him. He'd made that assertion right in front of her. Karen had killed her because, like Wade, Karen had likely seen how interested Sheryl was in the accusation. Tika, Jack, and Holly had all tried to reassure him, but he couldn't stop hearing Karen tell him that Sheryl's blood was on his hands.

As a news van parked at the edge of the yellow tape, Wade blew out his breath. He was running out of time. Before long, breaking news would be all over the local TV stations. Lawrence Butler's wife had been arrested at Wade's house. His parents couldn't learn about that on TV. Not after what they'd been through.

Finally, he connected the call and waited for someone to answer.

He smiled slightly at the sound of his dad's voice coming through the phone. The man sounded older now than he had before Lisa's death. Aged in a way he hadn't been just a few months ago. Losing Lisa had taken a toll on all of them, but especially on his parents. As much as Wade had been hurting, he knew it was worse for them.

How was he going to break it to them that her death was over photos? Because an overly ambitious wife didn't want her chances of moving to DC ruined by an overly ambitious freelance journalist.

Though Wade had been convinced from the start that Lisa's death hadn't been a simple accident, now that he knew the truth, his heart felt raw. The last moments of her life must have been terrifying. No matter what she may have done during her career, she hadn't deserved her life to end like that. She didn't deserve her life to be cut short by a crazed Karen Butler fighting over her camera.

Wade hated that he was going to have to tell his parents all these things. But that was a conversation they would have face-to-face. For now, he just needed to reassure them that he was okay so they didn't worry about him more than necessary.

"Hey, Dad," he said after clearing his throat.

"It's a bit late. Everything okay?"

"Actually, something happened tonight, and I wanted to tell you so you don't hear it on the news."

"Are you okay?" his dad asked, his voice spiked with fear.

"What happened?" Wade's mother asked in the background. Like his father, her voice seemed much more frail these days.

Wade glanced up, sensing eyes on him. Seeing Tika look at him with concern filled his chest with heavy, unnamed emotions, and he had to swallow hard. Reality was starting to sink in, and he noticed his hand trembling. He could have died tonight. Like Lisa. Tika could have died.

All so that woman could dangle off the arm of a congressman. Who knows how many more people she would have hurt to push her husband along the path to becoming more? Who knows how many more people she hurt to get him to where he was now? Was Lisa the first person who stood in her way? Or were there others who she "accidentally" got rid of so Lawrence Butler's star could rise?

Wade wasn't sure he wanted to know.

"Son?" his father asked. "What happened?"

He closed his eyes, and the words tumbled out of him. A confrontation. A shot fired. No one was hurt. He was okay. He promised he was okay.

"Why in the world would this woman shoot at you?" his mother asked.

In that moment, Wade wanted to tell her everything. That sense of an inner child seeking the comfort of a mother was almost overwhelming, but he resisted. When he told them that Lisa wasn't alone when she fell, he needed to be there to comfort them as well.

"We'll know more tomorrow," Wade said. "I'll come by first thing. But the police are still here—"

"We're coming over," his dad said.

"No, Dad. There isn't anything you can do tonight. I'm

fine. I wasn't hurt. I promise. Things here are just insane. There are crowds and police and news crews. You'd never make it to the house anyway. I wanted you to know before you saw it on TV or someone called to ask what happened."

"I still don't understand what happened," his mom said.

Wade smiled, clearly seeing the frustration that was likely plastered across her face. "Me neither, Mom. I'll be over first thing in the morning so we can try to make sense of it all."

"We love you," his dad said.

Emotion nearly choked Wade as he said, "Love you too."

As soon as he hung up, he noticed Tika coming toward him. His heart seemed to beat easier just having her closer to him. "How are you?" he asked as she neared him.

"I'm good. What about you?"

He shrugged. "In shock still, I guess."

"It's a lot to take in."

He looked beyond her to Holly and Jack. Holly cast a curious glance their way but was quickly distracted when a police officer called out to Jack.

"Any updates?" Wade asked.

Tika shook her head. "As soon as Dylan was told that Karen had been arrested, he caved and admitted she was the one who had given him the camera. She made him lots of big promises if he kept it for her."

"Does that make him an accessory?"

"That's up to the DA. I'm sure they'll cut him a deal for talking." She rested her hand on his knee, but only for a moment. He noticed how she glanced toward Holly, like a teen expecting to be caught by a parent. Clearly she hadn't told her boss that there was something going on between them.

Wade nearly smiled, but the weight of the situation was too much. Any other time, he would have teased her for keeping them a secret, though he understood why she would. He didn't know Holly well, but she seemed fairly straight-laced. Wade had no idea what she'd do if she found out Tika and Wade had started dating while he was paying their firm for her investigative talents.

"I'm sorry I didn't trust your instincts sooner," Tika said. "You knew all along that there was more to what happened to your sister, and I didn't believe you. I'm sorry."

Wade shook his head. "There was no evidence, Tika. You were going on facts. I get that."

"Even so, I should have been more open to what you were thinking." She smiled. "You were the one who kept saying this was about Lawrence Butler. I just couldn't put the pieces together."

"Yeah, but I never pegged his wife as a psycho."

Tika grew quiet. "Were you talking to your parents?"

"Yeah."

"How are they?"

He blew out his breath. "Concerned. I didn't tell them about Lisa. I need to do that in person, but I couldn't let them hear about all this on the news."

She nodded her understanding. "This is some mess, huh?"

"Yeah. But I'm glad it's done."

"Me too."

Sitting silently, they waited as hours passed, and the night grew darker and cooler. Slowly the crowd dispersed, the media stopped shouting questions, and the police disappeared. Holly and Jack left them alone with a reminder to Wade to avoid the press and stay out of sight as much as possible the next few days. Jack promised to be in touch with any updates, and Holly gave Tika one last suspicious look before they finally walked away.

"She knows we're together," Tika said. Her distressed tone confirmed what Wade had guessed—she hadn't told her boss about them.

Wade didn't bother to try to reassure her. He thought Holly had seen through them as well. "Is that going to be a problem?"

"No, but I would have liked to have told her before she figured it out."

Standing, he held his hand out waiting for her to take it. Once she did, he pulled her to her feet and led her inside. He closed and locked the door before turning and embracing her, squeezing her tight.

"Are you okay?" she asked.

"I will be. How are you?"

"Starting to feel a little stiff." Leaning back, she grinned slyly. "Did you see me kick her ass?"

"I did," he said with a smile. "It was hot."

"Yeah?"

"Hell yeah."

Her smile faded, and sympathy filled her eyes. Wade had known they'd have to discuss the reality of what they'd learned at some point, but he wasn't sure he wanted to do that just yet. Leaning down, he kissed her before she could ask how he was really doing. The kiss lingered, but when he tried to deepen it, she pulled back.

"Don't try to distract me," she whispered. "I'm worried about you."

"I know you are," he said, "but I'm okay. As okay as I can be."

Tilting her head, she sighed. "I'm here for you, Wade. Whatever you need to help you get through this."

"Thank you." Putting his hands on her hips, he pulled her to him. "I need that distraction I was after."

"I'm not sure the distraction you were after is a healthy coping skill."

He dipped his head and kissed the side of her neck. "Healthy coping skills are for losers."

Tika giggled and ran her hands over his chest. Pulling her with him, Wade walked into the bedroom. Closing the door, he left the stress of the evening behind them so he could focus on the woman in his arms.

[12]

TIKA SIGHED as she looked at the receptionist desk at HEARTS. The new receptionist was a woman named Susan. She'd been a victim of stalking some time ago. Holly had helped her but not before Susan had been taken and assaulted by the man infatuated with her.

Tika had no doubt Susan was up for the task of being their receptionist, and she knew how important it was to Holly to take care of the woman. Tika should have known that Susan would end up working at HEARTS at some point. Apparently she was ready to get back to living her life, and now she had a job to do so—one where Holly could look out for her.

"Are you our new go-to gal?" Tika asked, forcing a smile that she didn't feel. Not seeing Sam sitting there wasn't right, and that had absolutely nothing to do with Susan.

Susan smiled warmly, a kind of sweet motherly smile that wasn't common around the HEARTS office. The investigators were kind, of course, and Alexa had a way of being sisterly and supportive, but motherly? Nope. That was definitely something that had been missing in their little world. Though she was disappointed that Sam and Holly were both too damn stubborn to put their anger aside, Tika was glad Susan would be there to welcome her every day.

"Good morning," Susan said. "I'm only at this for a while, it seems. I've been warned that once Sam comes to her senses, I'll probably be relegated to some other position."

"Did Holly say that?" Tika asked, feeling hope that at least one of the women was coming to her senses.

"Rene, actually. Holly doesn't seem to be holding out any expectation that Sam will return."

Disappointment tugged at Tika. "Well, we'll see how things go." She walked to her office and set her tote bag down on her desk before heading down the hallway to Holly's office. Leaning against the door frame, Tika crossed her arms.

"How are you feeling?" Holly asked without looking away from her computer screen.

"A little stiff, but I'll survive. Any update on Karen?"

"She's trying to claim Lisa's death was an accident, but since she left the scene of said accident with Lisa's camera, her defense is fairly weak. Not to mention, once the ballistics evidence comes back on Sheryl Hunter, I think it's safe to say the gun will be tied to the one she pulled on you and Wade. She's not getting out of jail anytime soon."

"That's good to hear. I know Wade and his parents will be relieved."

Holly's eyes turned curious. "Speaking of Wade..."

Tika opened her mouth to admit the shift in their relationship, but Holly didn't give her a chance to speak.

"You two seemed close."

Tika's heart fluttered a bit. She didn't think Holly would chastise her, but she still felt guilty admitting the truth. "We are. Very close."

"Dating?"

"Yeah," she said as an unexpected sense of apprehension rolled down her spine.

After what seemed like several tension-filled hours, Holly nodded. "He seems nice. There wasn't anything in his background check to be concerned about. But I'll dig deeper now."

Tika would have laughed if that came from anyone other than Holly. She knew the woman well enough to know she wasn't joking. She was going to turn over every rock Wade Steele had ever looked at just to make sure Tika was in good hands.

"Thanks," she said because there was no point in protesting. "Have you apologized to Sam yet?"

Holly leaned back in her chair and eyed Tika. "She went too far."

"I know she did. I talked to her about that. I think she gets it now."

"So why should I apologize? She's the one who tried to steamroll me out of my own wedding."

"Because you're the bigger person."

Holly laughed dryly. "While true, that doesn't mean I'm apologizing. She has no respect for anyone, Tika. I've tolerated her immaturity for longer than I should have because I kept waiting for her to grow up. I adore her as a person, but she cannot work here when she continually breaks the rules, and she absolutely cannot plan my wedding when she has repeatedly proven that she has no respect for what Jack and I want."

After walking farther into Holly's office, Tika dropped into a chair and lowered her voice as to not be overheard. "So Susan is here to stay?"

"Yup."

"Can she hack into email accounts?"

Holly pressed her lips together and shook her head. "All that illegal activity is reason number five thousand and one why Sam shouldn't be here. She was going to get us into trouble someday."

"That illegal activity has saved the day more times than I can count."

Holly looked away as she took a deep breath. She couldn't argue that, but she seemed to be searching for a reason to.

"We need her, Holly," Tika said softly. "We need Sam on this team as much as we need anyone else."

"I've been telling her that," came a raspy voice with a hint of a Brooklyn accent. Rene walked into the room and dropped a file on Holly's desk before putting her hands on her hips.

"I thought she listened to you," Tika said.

Rene scowled at Holly. "Only when I agree with her."

"That's not true," Holly said. "I take your advice all the time."

"Bullshit," Rene muttered.

"Call her," Tika stated.

"Call her," Rene repeated.

"Just fucking call her," Eva called from across the hall.

Holly rolled her eyes and squeezed out between her clenched teeth, "Fine. Get out, and I'll call her."

"About time," Rene said.

"Close the door on your way out," Holly insisted when Rene and Tika high-fived each other.

"She's calling," Tika assured Eva.

"Thank God. Nothing against Susan," Eva quickly added. "I adore her, but we need Sam back."

"None of us have anything against Susan," Rene said. "We'll find a place for her."

"We could always make Sam a full-time cyber investigator," Tika said. "We need one of those."

Rene considered that for a moment. "Let's get those two back on even ground, then we'll talk to them about it. I think getting Sam back here is the first step."

"Agree," Alexa said, squeezing between Tika and Rene to get into Eva's office. Without asking, she rounded the desk and opened Eva's top drawer. As she looked inside, she frowned. "Where are your cookies?"

"You ate them all," Eva said. "PMS must be kicking your ass this month."

"No, my period isn't..." Alexa said and then stood straight up as she widened her eyes. The oxygen seemed to leave the room. "What's the date?" she asked but didn't wait for anyone to answer. She leaned close to Eva's computer, and her eyes got even wider. "Uh-oh."

"Uh-oh?" Eva asked.

"Uh-oh," Rene muttered.

Tika, by contrast, smiled brightly. "Yay."

"She didn't answer my call," Holly said, coming out of her

office. She stopped in the hallway, peering in at her team between Rene and Tika. "Why are you all crammed in here like sardines?"

"Alexa's late," Rene said.

"I didn't say that," Alexa stated.

"She ate all my cookies," Eva said.

"Are you pregnant?" Holly asked.

Tika's smile widened. "She's so pregnant."

"I didn't say that," Alexa stated again.

Eva stood. "Come on. Let's go to the drug store and get a test and more cookies."

Alexa put her hand low on her stomach. "And chips?"

"And chips," Eva added.

Tika pulled her phone from her pocket when the device pinged to let her know she had a message. She smiled when she read Wade's plea for her to hurry...and to bring a bottle of red wine with her since he forgot to buy one.

"That's some smile," Eva said, distracting her.

Shoving her phone back into her pocket, Tika took a deep breath. "Um. It was Wade. We're having dinner tonight. We're kind of...dating now," she said, dreading the response of her coworkers.

"Damn it," Rene spat out in her signature accent.

Tika jolted. Okay, she didn't think they'd be thrilled, but that wasn't exactly what she was hoping for.

Eva, by contrast, giggled and did a little dance before holding out her hand. Alexa pulled cash out of her pocket and deposited it into Eva's palm.

"I'll take my winnings now," Eva said to Rene.

Rene shook her head and frowned at Tika. "I was

counting on you to resist temptation, kid." She dug cash out of her pocket and slapped it into Eva's palm.

As she started to realize what was happening, Tika's jaw dropped. "I can't believe you guys."

"Talk to Sam," Eva said, accepting her win. "She started the pool."

"Yeah, I'll do that." Tika's frown was almost as drastic as Rene's. "Nothing is sacred around here."

"No, it's not," Rene said, and her frown turned into a soft smile. "Make sure you tell him to treat you right. We don't want to hurt him."

"But we will," Eva offered.

"I'll be sure to let him know. I'm heading out. I have a date," she said with a smile before leaving her coworkers to whatever bet they planned on making next—which would likely be on the results of Alexa's pregnancy test.

Wade shook the match to extinguish it after lighting a candle sitting in the middle of his table. He'd never been the romantic kind, but he wanted to do this for Tika. He wanted her to know his feelings for her weren't limited to her investigation. He felt so much more.

It wasn't love. Not yet. But it could be. He could definitely see them building a future together. He jumped when the timer in the kitchen beeped loudly. Laughing lightly at himself, Wade tried to shake off the jitters that had followed him around all day.

The image of Karen wielding a gun had haunted him in

his sleep and during his waking hours. So had the vision of Lisa falling down the stairs. Screaming. Landing dead at the bottom.

Closing his eyes, Wade silently cursed his mind for going down that road again. "Stop it," he whispered harshly to himself.

After taking a few deep breaths, he opened the oven and pulled out the lasagna he'd baked. The dinner was home-made-ish. He hadn't put the layers of pasta, sauce, and cheese together, but he had bought the dinner from his grocery store's freezer section and baked it. That was close enough. Or so he told himself.

Maybe he'd learn to make a lasagna sometime, but that wasn't going to happen anytime soon. He had too much on his mind these days. He was struggling to find his footing more than he'd wanted to admit. He supposed that was the feeling that drove him to push Tika to help him dig into Lisa's death.

Without his sister, he felt like he was in free fall. That had eased some when he was searching for the truth about her death. Now that he had it, he felt himself falling again. He hadn't realized how much he missed their talks until it really started sinking in that he'd never have that again.

He was glad he had Tika, though. He knew she could help him heal. Already, he had a tendency to seek her out when he felt overwhelmed by the stress of his life. That was a heck of a burden to put on someone he had barely started a relationship with, but the bond he felt with her was strong. He was certain she felt the same. The way she had constantly sought him out the night before when the house was buzzing with activity made him certain she felt just as strongly for him.

He smiled when the phone in his back pocket buzzed. Pulling it free, he confirmed what he suspected. Tika was texting him to let him know she was there. By the time he rushed to the front door, she was walking up the sidewalk. His smile widened as he watched her close in on him.

Her hair was free, hanging loose around her shoulders. The way he liked it.

"Hey," she said with a smooth voice full of promise of what was to come.

His heart warmed, and his blood pressure spiked with anticipation. "Hey." Reaching out, he grabbed her hand and pulled her to him, greeting her with a long, deep kiss, making his own promises. "Just in time for dinner."

She walked in and inhaled deeply. "Smells great."

"Lasagna," he offered. "I hope you like lasagna."

"I do. How are you parents?" she asked as he led her into the dining room.

"They're okay. They took the news better than I thought they would."

Tika's smile widened when she noticed the table. "Wow. Look at this. Very fancy."

Wade pulled out a chair and helped her sit before planting a kiss on her cheek. "I'm seducing you," he whispered.

"You don't have to," she whispered back.

"But I want to." He kissed her cheek one more time before filling her wine glass. "Stay put. I'll be right back."

He rushed into the kitchen and served up two slices of

the lasagna before carrying the plates back to the dining room. "How's the wine?"

"Delicious."

"Good." He sat a plate in front of her. "Bon appétit."

Sitting across from her, he draped a napkin over his lap. "How was your day?"

"Well, I wrapped up the paperwork on our case, and Holly still hasn't apologized to Sam. Oh, and Alexa may or may not be with child."

"Wow. Heck of a day," he said as he cut into his dinner. He took a big bite and nearly spit it out. The noodles were hard, the sauce way too sweet, and the chunks of meat were questionable. He looked across the table at Tika. Though she hadn't said anything, he noticed that she hadn't taken a second bite. "This is terrible, isn't it?"

Tika started to shake her head but then nodded. "Yeah, it's kinda bad."

"Okay, so I'm not a great cook, but I tried. I mean," he gestured around the table, "I put all this together."

"And it's beautiful."

"I'll order in next time."

She laughed lightly. "That's okay. I didn't come for the food."

He lifted his brows. "No?"

"No."

Warmth filled his chest and settled low in his gut. "What'd ya come for?"

"The entertainment," she said with a sly smile.

"Whatcha thinking?" he asked, already knowing.

Licking her lip, she simply grinned at him before standing

and taking a step back from the table. A sly grin curled her lips as she ran her hand down the front of her shirt, releasing the buttons that held it closed one by one.

Wade inhaled slowly as he watched her slip the shirt off, revealing the deliciously soft flesh of her shoulders and the white-lace bra she wore. She smiled when he took off his shirt and tossed it aside. A slight grin found his face as he slid down onto the plush sofa, his body already reacting to her. One by one, she kicked off her high-heeled shoes and lost several inches to her height as she reached for the button of her slacks.

Wade swallowed, trying to control the racing of his heart and trembling of his hands as he watched Tika slowly slide her pants over her hips. His breath hitched when the material finally fell down her body, leaving her standing across the room in matching white lace and black stockings. Resting his head against his fingertips, he smiled slowly, waiting for her to come to him. She didn't disappoint him as she slowly walked across the room, staring at him with eyes full of desire.

Bringing his hand to his mouth, he ran his thumb over his lip, resisting the urge to reach out and pull her to him when she stopped just a few feet in front of him. Wade felt the throb of wanting when she lifted her leg and rested her foot between his legs. His eyes slowly lowered from hers, over her breasts and stomach to the leg that was in front of him. Inhaling slowly, he took in every inch of skin revealed as she slowly pushed the stocking down her leg before tossing it aside and putting her bare foot back to the floor, only to repeat the painful process with the other leg.

He finally gave into the urge to touch her and ran his

hands over the flesh she had just revealed to him until his hands rested on her hips. Slowly moving his eyes up her body, he sighed when they fell on her face. Pulling her forward a step, he urged her closer until she straddled him and sat on his lap. Leaning forward to kiss her, his lips quivered when she sat back slightly, refusing to let him.

Tika smiled as she reached up and ran her fingers along the side of his face. Her breath quickened when he brushed his nose along her cheek before sitting back and watching her face as she worked her magic on him. A moment later, he felt the scorch of her touch as her hands ran over his chest. She inhaled deeply as his bare chest pressed against hers and felt his hot breath on her neck, then ran her hands up his bare arms, over his shoulders and down his chest.

Wade shifted slightly beneath her as she unbuckled his belt and popped open the button of his slacks. Sliding his hands up her back, he released the clasp of her bra and sighed as he slowly pushed the material down her arms, releasing her breasts. Slowly leaning forward, he ran his nose up the length of her neck until he found her ear and released a shaky breath as she pressed her bare chest to his.

He longed to feel what was teasing him, taste the flesh that taunted him, but he resisted as his hands slid back up her arms and cupped her head. He stared into her eyes, deep into her soul, willing her to know the depth of his longing before slowly pulling her to him. When their lips finally met, the passion exploded, and the game was over. The sensation of her nibbling at his mouth sent him over the edge, and Wade knew he had to have what he had been missing or risk going completely insane.

With one swift movement, he lifted her off his lap and laid her back on the sofa, his body instantly on top of hers, his mouth burning kisses along her neck, breathing her name and swearing his love for her in between. By the time they finished undressing, both were in a heated rush to feel the other's body melting against them. There was no time wasted touching or tasting as he quickly entered her, sighing with relief when he felt her body welcome his with a wet heat he would never tire of.

He was amazed that he didn't instantly climb to the top of their love as she did but kept his control, moving slowly with deliberate strokes as he ran his hands through her hair, kissed every inch of her face, and spoke softly of his devotion. When he finally did get to the point of no return, he slid his hand down her body to her hip and lifted her slightly, urging her legs to close tighter around him. Grinding his teeth together, he buried his face in her neck, fighting the scream that had been building within him.

Finally relaxing, he slid beside her and pulled her close to him, both gasping for breath as he pulled the blanket off the back of the couch, covering their naked bodies. Tucking her in his arms, he kissed her shoulder and inhaled the scent of her perfume. He smiled when she whispered that she would always love him and never leave him, repeating the same in her ear, he closed his eyes, knowing that they would definitely be building a future together.

Present day...

Estrada Investigations was like HEARTS Investigative Services. Except...not quite.

E.I. reeked of testosterone and moderately priced cologne. The cases weren't nearly as interesting, and the investigators weren't nearly as quick to jump in on topics like Hollywood breakups, the best mascara, or the latest fashion.

Even so, Samantha Turner was determined to make the most of her new position as a cyber investigator at E.I. Victor Estrada was giving her an amazing opportunity, and she wasn't going to blow it—despite her history of blowing things. Her latest blow job, as she liked to call her missteps in life, was pissing her former boss off so much that she had to find new employment.

Sam never thought she'd leave her job as the computer guru and ultimate research nerd for HEARTS. She'd loved working with the all-female team of private investigators.

They had gone from coworkers to friends to basically being sisters. However, nothing Sam ever did seemed to make her boss happy. *Former* boss.

Sam was far too light and airy for Holly's deep, dark, soulless outlook on life. They didn't have the same taste in men, clothes, or jokes. Holly actually didn't have any taste for jokes. She was about as amused by Sam as a bear in shackles. Sam had worked around that for as long as she could.

However, when Holly announced her engagement, Sam had forgotten just how oil-and-water their relationship could be. She was desperate to help Holly have an amazing wedding. And that had been the beginning of the end.

Holly had never been known for having a soft side, but Sam finally got fed up with Holly's blatant disrespect for her and her work and quit during one of their heated confrontations.

Though Sam was heartbroken to leave her coworkers, within days of leaving that job, she landed on her feet at Estrada Investigations. Despite pleas from her former teammates to make amends with Holly and return to HEARTS, Sam no longer felt she belonged on their team.

And she was confident she had found her dream job as a cyber investigator. Holly would have *never* given her that kind of responsibility. And Sam was excited to have an opportunity to prove herself—mostly as a *told you so* to Holly.

Rolling her shoulders back, Sam pushed thoughts of her old job from her mind and held her head high as she walked into Estrada Investigations. While she had loved her job at HEARTS, this was the first job where she was an equal.

Of sorts.

Victor's younger brother, Javier, and their friend and fellow investigator Conner O'Riley were definitely higher on the food chain than their latest addition, but Sam was definitely more than the go-to gofer that she'd been at her last job.

Even though the atmosphere wasn't quite the same at E.I., and she had to keep more of her sarcastic comments to herself than she liked, she enjoyed the job. She enjoyed being valued for what she brought to the table. Sure, she'd only been with E.I. for like a week and still didn't have her first real case, but she still felt more valued. She still felt like part of the team.

"Good morning," she said to Lorraine, the woman who occupied the reception desk.

Sam made it a point to be extra nice to Lorraine because she, herself, had spent far too much of her time at HEARTS being overlooked by clients because she was "just the receptionist." She wanted to make doubly sure that Lorraine knew she and her hard work were appreciated. But also because Lorraine was so maternal and kind, there was no other way to respond to her.

The older woman smiled warmly. "There are donuts in the conference room for the meeting this morning."

Sam perked up. Though she tried to keep her diet on the healthier side of the line, there was no better way to start the day than a sweet pastry and a large cup of coffee.

"Oh, what's the special occasion?"

Lorraine grinned and winked. "Victor's been in an unusually good mood lately. He brought them in."

While Sam and Victor Estrada had never been anything but professional in their ten or so days of knowing each other, there was an undercurrent of something going on there. When she'd walked into E.I. for her interview with her heart racing from anxiety, the last thing she'd expected was to walk out with her heart racing because she was in lust. She could barely remember a thing about her interview.

She remembered Lorraine had walked her into the conference room. She remembered shaking three men's hands, but she only remembered looking at Victor. In fact, she had left the interview and gone straight to the closest ice cream shop to console herself because she was certain staring at the man who owned the company like he was a scoop of butter pecan was not the best way to get a job.

However, the man in question had called her the next day to offer her the job. Even better, he had asked her to start as soon as possible.

Ever since her first day, Sam had had an awfully hard time tearing her gaze away from his almost-black eyes, tanned skin, and the way his muscles rippled beneath his designer shirts.

Feeling warmth rush to her cheeks as she thought of the man who had apparently brought in donuts, she gave her head a hard shake. She was not going to get involved with her boss. Doing so would just prove Holly right. Holly had continually insisted that Sam would never be an investigator because she refused to take the work seriously. She refused to put the case above whatever else came along.

Despite what Holly might have thought, private investigators didn't have to be sticks in the damn mud. They could have lives, and even enjoy them. But Sam was not going to jump into bed with her new boss and prove a point Holly was likely sitting back and waiting on—that Sam would fail without Holly there to save her.

Unfortunately, though, the electricity that sparked between Sam and Victor whenever they were in the same room was already causing her problems. Their coworkers had picked up on the undeniable attraction between them, and while Lorraine seemed pleased, Conner and Javier gave Sam the same frowns and disapproving looks she used to get from her former boss.

So, no, Sam would not act on her attraction to Victor. No, she would not trip and fall. And, hell no, she would not screw up this new job over a man.

Nope. Not going to happen.

"Maybe he got a puppy or something," Sam said before walking away, doing what she could to dismiss the notion that his good mood had anything to do with her.

"Or something," Lorraine called after her.

Sam walked into her office—*her* office—and placed her bag on her desk. This was the first time she had a space to call her own. The reception desk at HEARTS had simply been a spot for her to sit. That hadn't been her space. She couldn't keep photos or other personal items there. Holly was far too paranoid. She'd said that by putting out personal information, even a photograph, Sam was making herself vulnerable to the people who came and went. While most of those people were clients, Holly's ability to trust them was limited. Her ability to trust *anyone* was limited.

Sam had attempted to sneak some personal items into the area, but unfortunately for her, several of her other coworkers had agreed with Holly. Her workspace had been sterile because the women that she'd worked with were convinced someone, somewhere, someday was going to get fixated on their receptionist and stalk her or something.

However, this was *her* office. *Her* space.

She smiled as she ran her fingers over the framed photo of her and Tika that she'd put on her desk her first day at E.I. Tika was her closest friend. She was also an investigator at HEARTS. Of all of Sam's former coworkers, it was Tika who had begged Sam to make amends with Holly the most. The day Sam had stormed out of the HEARTS office, swearing she'd never go back, Tika had shown up at Sam's place with a bottle of wine, a pint of ice cream, and sad eyes.

They'd both cried, but Sam was determined that she'd done the right thing. Unless Holly apologized for being so harsh, Sam wouldn't go back. So far, Holly hadn't apologized, and Sam hadn't gone back. Now she had a new job that she was confident would be the perfect fit for her.

"Good morning," Victor said from the doorway.

Sam smiled as she met his gaze.

He didn't bother being casual about skimming over her suit. "You look nice today."

"As do you."

He smiled and winked. "Meeting starts in five. Better grab a donut and fill your mug before the guys get in there."

Then he was gone.

Just like at HEARTS, the team members at Estrada had a morning meeting every day to catch up. Unlike HEARTS, this team wasn't all women. Actually, Sam was the only female investigator at the moment. Victor handled cold cases. He enjoyed trying to solve puzzles that no one else could.

Jordan worked pretty much whatever came his way. And Sam was their new cyber investigator.

Tika used to say that Sam could find anything ever looked at on the Internet. That was only a slight exaggeration. Sam knew how to find things. How to get into places where she shouldn't be, and how to do so without being detected.

Holly hadn't always appreciated Sam's abilities, but she suspected her new team would—once they decided to give her a chance. Unfortunately for Sam, she had a way of shooting herself in the foot, and that happened on the first day of her new position when it became obvious there was an attraction between her and her new boss.

Victor clearly didn't have a problem blurring the lines, but Sam was trying to do the right thing, damn it. This was her fresh start. Her chance to prove herself. And she feared she was already fumbling it. But she never had been very good at doing the right thing—at least not for herself.

"Focus," she muttered quietly when she was alone. She was a week into this job. Today might be the day. She might get her first case. Once she did, she was going to be nose to the damn grindstone. Laser focused. Singularly orientated. Nothing...and she meant *absolutely nothing*...was going to distract her.

Especially a man.

Determined to stand by her convictions, Sam walked into the conference room with her notebook in hand and went right to the snack table. She filled a cup with hot coffee, snagged a Long John, and took a seat as far from that tall drink of temptation as she could get. Which, unfortunately, wasn't nearly far enough. She was still tempted to crawl across the table and curl up in his lap.

Shit.

Victor couldn't remember the last time he'd had such a hard time focusing around a woman, but damn if Samantha Turner hadn't turned his world upside down the day she'd walked in for an interview. Though Javier and Conner had sat in the interview with him, he hadn't given them a chance to speak. He'd known he'd hire that woman as soon as she'd shaken his hand—qualifications be damned. Something about her made him want her there, with him, even if she hadn't been worth hiring.

Which he'd decided she hadn't been after reading her résumé again after she'd accepted the job.

His teammates had given him hell for hiring her based on her looks, but he was the boss. Or so he'd reminded them. He'd be concerned about sexual harassment just from the way he looked at her if she weren't looking at him the same way. She wanted him just as much and was just as open about it, and that had thrown him for a loop. She didn't seem interested in playing games or teasing.

He wasn't sure exactly what she was interested in, but he was eager to find out.

CONTINUE HEARTS SERIES WITH RUNAWAY HEARTS

The Women of HEARTS Series Book Six

Seducing Kate

A Life Without Water

As a teen, Marci Bolden skipped over young adult books and jumped right into reading romance novels. She never left.

Marci lives in the Midwest with her husband, kiddos, and numerous rescue pets. If she had an ounce of willpower, Marci would embrace healthy living, but until cupcakes and wine are no longer available at the local market, she will appease her guilt by reading self-help books and promising to join a gym "soon."

Visit her here:
www.marcibolden.com

facebook.com/MarciBoldenAuthor
x.com/BoldenMarci
instagram.com/marciboldenauthor

www.ingramcontent.com/pod-product-compliance
Lightning Source LLC
Chambersburg PA
CBHW061237210726